SEEN READING

SEEN READING

Julie Wilson

freehand books

© *Julie Wilson 2012*

All rights reserved. No part of this publication may be reproduced, stored in a retrieval system, or transmitted in any form or by any means, graphic, electronic, or mechanical — including photocopying, recording, taping, or through the use of information storage and retrieval systems — without prior written permission of the publisher or, in the case of photocopying or other reprographic copying, a licence from the Canadian Copyright Licensing Agency (Access Copyright), One Yonge Street, Suite 800, Toronto, ON, Canada, M5E 1E5.

Freehand Books gratefully acknowledges the support of the Canada Council for the Arts for its publishing program. ¶ Freehand Books, an imprint of Broadview Press Inc., acknowledges the financial support for its publishing program provided by the Government of Canada through the Canada Book Fund.

 Canada Council for the Arts   Conseil des Arts du Canada

Freehand Books
515 – 815 1st Street SW   Calgary, Alberta   T2P 1N3
www.freehand-books.com

Book orders: LitDistCo
100 Armstrong Avenue   Georgetown, Ontario   L7G 5S4
Telephone: 1-800-591-6250   Fax: 1-800-591-6251
orders@litdistco.ca
www.litdistco.ca

Library and Archives Canada Cataloguing In Publication

Wilson, Julie, 1969–
Seen reading / Julie Wilson.

Short stories.
ISBN 978-1-55481-079-6

I. Title.

PS8645.I469S44 2012   C813'.6   C2012-900305-0

Edited by Robyn Read
Book design by Natalie Olsen, www.kisscutdesign.com
Author photo by Derek Wuenschirs

Printed on FSC recycled paper and bound in Canada

FOR YOU.

CONTENTS

PROLOGUE   xi

Regret had never been the thing he did, but the thing he did next.

Tin Can	2
After Joe Brainard	4
Undertow	6
Cherry Tree	8
Girl's Dorm	10
A Quick Peek	12
One Boy In	14
Dress Rehearsal	16
(In)digestion	18
Legal Limits	20
He Didn't See It Coming	22

She'd thought no pain, no joy, was exempt from fading, until this lingered.

Breaking Ties	26
Six Spin	28
Morning Glories	30
House Rules	32
Complementary Colours	34
Surplus	36
Small Talks	38

Lots and Lots	40
Woman and Parrot	42
Dreams of a Would-Be Government Employee	44
Simple Sandwiches	46

*Soon her son will have nine teeth and know how to walk,
the memory of eight teeth a distant luxury.*

Tho. Shelton	50
Bagged Lunch	52
Miss Popular	54
Riding the Rails	56
It Begins the Same	58
Pillow Talk	60
The Health Hustle	62
Swedish Berries	64
Mercy	66
Clearcutting	68

What had their love been if not the exception?

Love Noted	72
Ends	74
The Young Lovers, Part I	76
The Young Lovers, Part II	78
Biopsy	80
Cherry	82
Love Will Tear Us Apart	84
Divorced Before Thirty	86
Flat	88
Side Tables	90

The temptation of her acceptance, a lure.

Sticks and Twigs	94
Intrusion	96
Simmer	98
Cursive	100
Winter Wonderland	102
Indiana Summers	104
Pinhead	106
'86	108
Jelly	110
Red	112
Visitor	114

For rent: white wedding.

Irlsgay	118
A Room of His Own	120
Sugar Bowls	122
Esther	124
If This Buick Could Talk	126
Grace	128
Creature Feature	130

The more things strayed, the more they stayed the strange.

Girlfriends	134
The Curious Collector	136
Sailor	138
Reception	140

Like Mother, Like Son	142
Glory, Glory	144
Rumble Row	146
Put to Pasture	148
Of Age	150
When You Least Expect It	152
Secret Santa	154

To have and to scold, toward a day far worse, or better.

XXX-XXX-XXXX	158
Monsters in the Bones	160
Wedding Dress	162
Wearing Her Indoor Face	164
Pricks	166
Counting Cars	168
Procession	170
The Birth of a Handsome Nose	172
Pink	174
Hero	176
Holding	178
Twisty Ties	180

SEEN READING	183
ACKNOWLEDGEMENTS	189

PROLOGUE

I'm a literary voyeur. Like the wanderer who steps off the predictable path, I set out most days in the hope that I'll encounter a new way of seeing the spaces in which I live. I'm also a collector. Years ago, I began to collect sightings of readers, because I thought I might gain awareness of how our urban lives are mapped out in the books we choose to read in public, particularly on transit. Many people, for instance, read on transit to place a wall between themselves and fellow passengers; others don't know how to be alone in a crowd. For the rest of us, that commute is the only time we get to retreat into an extended private conversation with ourselves as we dive into another's world.

A question began to persist: If I'm a voyeur, are you, the reader, an exhibitionist? How do readers *perform* the private act of reading within the public realm, their preference for the written word on full display. The book becomes an invitation to look closer. And, just think, you have no idea what emotions may floor you from one sentence to the next, and when they do, I'm there, watching. I began to imagine who each reader might be, and how the text they read would ultimately impact the spaces in which they live.

The reader sighting that started it all was at The Old Nick on Danforth Avenue. At the bar, a woman neared the end of a book. Visibly distraught, she placed the book down from time to time, only to pick it up again moments later. This continued for some time, until she stood suddenly, slapping her money on the bar as she readied to leave. She was so distressed, in fact, that I asked if she was all right, noting the title of the book before it disappeared into her bag. She said that this wasn't the right time or place to end the book, that when it came time to say goodbye to the protagonist she'd need to be at home. After she left, I ran to the nearest bookstore where I purchased a copy of the book she'd been reading: *A Complicated Kindness* by Miriam Toews. I read it that night in anticipation of the final pages, where I would once again meet this reader within the book that moved her so.

I began to look for readers everywhere. You may be the woman I see who, each week, is deeper into yet another book. You may be the man whose weathered copies of science fiction novels betray multiple readings. It's likely that the book you carry bears the splatter of last night's dinner or the crumbs of this morning's breakfast, the vague odour of your bed sheets or your partner's cologne. Under my observation, the reader both reads and reveals a narrative, the act of reading in turn inspiring an act of writing.

My work is performed on Toronto's subways, streetcars, and buses. In Toronto, transit riders are decidedly introverted. Courtesy aside — removing my knapsack so you can pass, standing up so you can sit, wearing fitted earphones so you don't have to hear my music — fellow passengers enter into an unspoken agreement that it's not rude to sit in silence, gesturing only in the rare instant that you're sitting on my jacket, or I'm standing on your purse strap. Perhaps this is why readers feel safe to pull out a book, turning the average subway car into a cultural cocoon. With little effort, the average forty-five minute trip yields at least twenty reader sightings.

During downtown Toronto rush hour, shoulder-to-shoulder I'm often able to note a book's title and author, and most often the page number at the time of the sighting. Armed with this information and only a brief physical description of the reader, I craft a fictional response to the entire scene, ending each sighting with a poetic short fiction about the reader and who he or she may be. The online blog *Seen Reading* — www.seenreading.com — is the forum in which I posted my reader sightings. To date, there are over seven hundred sightings, and the project earned me the moniker "Gossip Girl of the Book World" among my regular visitors. Early versions of some of the stories that appear here originated there.

The pieces are bite-sized, reflective of an age in which communications are disseminated through texts, tweets, and status updates. Twitter, for instance, places constraints on the user, one hundred and forty characters per tweet, to be exact. It's taught us how to be mindful of our words. In a venue where every character counts, complete words and entire sentences take on a whole new meaning. How and why we place importance on each character, word, and sentence becomes a craft. What's followed is an increase in the popularity in online microfiction, postcard fictions, poetic short fictions — whichever term you prefer. The economy of a tweet, by way of contrast, however, should not be mistaken for a creatively constrained art form. Take Ernest Hemingway's infamous short story: "For sale: baby shoes, never worn." When I read this the first time, I couldn't help but wonder if it was a sentence that had been cut from one of his novels, or a rushed scribble on a napkin intended as the starting point for another. Mostly, though, I wondered if the first draft had been seven words. Or seventeen. Do we say more when we say less?

I'm far from alone in my impulse, the Seen Reading Movement alive in any person who has ever wanted to ask a complete stranger how he or she is liking a book as they rumble down the track together to their final destinations. While commuters may feel anonymous on public transit, the vehicles are structured in such a way that we face one another, always in the line of someone else's view. Public transit situates us so that we are given license to accept what's right in front of us, but will likely arouse our desire to compare our narrative to someone else's, to give ourselves permission to speculate upon a person's private space, or life, with no fear of recourse or punishment. Where did you come from? How did you get here? Where are you going?

After five years of watching readers, I've arrived at the conclusion that as there is no one way to read a book, there is no one way to know a reader. To that end, I address each character only as He or She to invite many readings of the text.

Be seeing you.

Julie Wilson

How often have you sat in a restaurant, theatre,
or bus and wondered who the people around you are?
This novel will give you the illusion that you can know
— indeed, that you are Godlike and omniscient.
This can be a very pleasurable sensation.

Geoff Ryman, 253

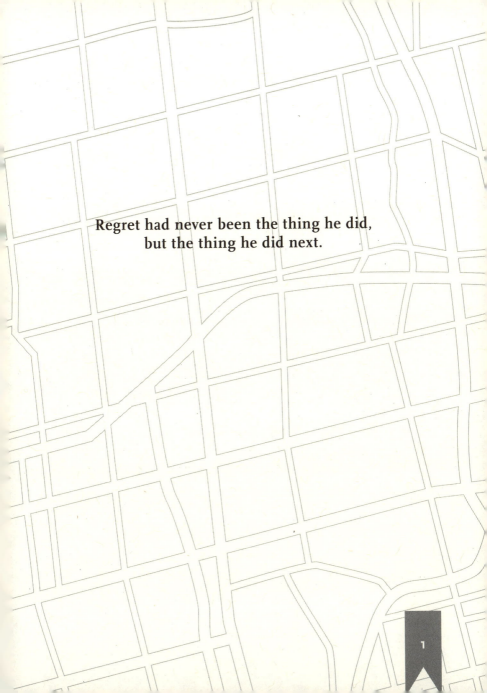

> Regret had never been the thing he did,
> but the thing he did next.

Tin Can

In the train tunnel for five minutes, a young mother has let her child go to the front. Here he presses his face to the glass inside cupped hands, eyes adjusting to the dark, bobbing headlamps crossing in the distance, workers on the track. The mother reads while the woman beside her watches a telenovela on a portable player, *Malhação* or *Patito Feo,* she wouldn't know.

The passengers get tense, the train showing no sign of moving. The banter from the soap opera is rapid-fire, the audio hollow and far away, like tiny people yelling inside a tin can. We are in a tin can, the mother thinks. What would our voices sound like from the next station? How much longer before we'll break down and talk to one another? She looks over the forearm of the woman to see what drama is unfolding. Her son jumps unsteadily on one foot, hands stuffed into his back pockets.

READER

Caucasian female, late 40s, with long blond hair,
wearing leather pants, black fleece,
and large gold necklace.

The World to Come
Dara Horn
(W.W. Norton, 2006)
P 10

After Joe Brainard

He remembers a bump to his forehead, the cat ten minutes before the alarm.

He remembers the police, thirty-one arrests, the deep voice on the clock radio sounding morning.

He remembers remembering, a surge in his stomach, reaching out for the cat. The cat is gone.

He remembers his bare toes touching the cold floor, how once it would be followed by a warm hand on the back of his neck.

He remembers the empty drawers, one less toothbrush, and the extra set of keys taking up space in his loose change bowl.

READER

East Indian male, 40s, with shaved head, wearing black wool coat, collar up, and blue striped scarf.

I Remember
Joe Brainard
(Granary Books, 2001)
P 117

Undertow

Breakfast was strawberry Pop Tarts. The boy and Uncle sat in the kitchen blowing on the filling, rolling the toasted pastry around in their mouths. Uncle threw his down on the paper towel, switching it out for coffee. The boy walked his fingers across the table and grabbed the leftover, holding it to his chest like he was planning to store it for the long season ahead. Uncle straightened to scold him, but the boy had started nipping away at the tart like a beast, revelling in his tiny victory.

He saw a glimpse of the boy's mother in those mischievous eyes.

He recalled living on the beach when they were young. His mother had called it a vacation, a summer down by the lake, but they'd lost their home and Mother was ill. He'd gone out into the surf, far too far, his sister's job to make sure he didn't go astray, but he giggled, wading further. A succession of waves had come in and he struggled to stay above water, sucked under and spit out, over and again, scanning the shore each time he broke the surface.

She would come get him. His sister would come get him.

When he finally came ashore safe, his sister was standing by the tent, their mother inside, fading, her eyes as murky as the lake water. His sister would raise him.

Uncle caught himself glaring at the boy. Lord in heaven, he thought. Please don't let the kid have it too.

READER

Caucasian male, mid-40s, with wide part in greying hair, wearing worn leather motorcycle jacket, black jeans, and brown hiking boots.

The Inheritance of Loss
Kiran Desai
(Penguin Canada, 2006)
P 56

Cherry Tree

It's late afternoon, almost time for dinner. She dangles a bottle of cream soda beside her, out of sight of her nearby daughter who plays beside the barn. She doesn't usually like carbonated beverages — cream soda is her daughter's treat — but she could use one now, something unexpected.

She acknowledges her neighbour, walking over from the next farm. She rents out all the land to him for cattle. She only wanted the barn. She raises her eyebrows in the direction of what's left of the cherry tree newly planted in memory of her late husband. Today, the bull arrived and she and her daughter stood near the electric fence to see which cow he would pick. He picked the cherry tree.

The neighbour inspects the tree's trunk, hopeful there's something he might do to make it better. Instead he nods and shrugs. She shrugs too. What can you do? He starts toward the porch, scratches the inside of his forearm. But then he thinks better of it, crossing back over the long field home, minding he doesn't lose his footing in a gopher hole.

Beside the barn, her daughter lies on the bench, legs up, arms outstretched, eyes shut, imagining what it would be like to fall through the clouds with no parachute, no place to land.

READER

Black female, early 30s, wearing sleek, long coat,
high boots, and black-framed glasses.

The Perfect Circle
Pascale Quiviger
Translated by Sheila Fischman
(Cormorant Books, 2006)
P 70

Girl's Dorm

She wakes up on her half of the twin bed. The dorm room sways with each tilt of her head. The roommate came in at some point, she remembers now, then left.

She pulls herself up against the wall and surveys the room in light, a *Rolling Stone* tear of Sinead O'Connor thumbtacked to the wall, curling at the edges. Balls of clothes, some of them hers.

The girl beside her is beautiful. Wavy dark hair, arms laced over her head, a Kafka T-shirt riding up to reveal her runner's core. An emptied twenty-sixer of lemon gin sits atop the bar fridge, their first mistake, a tray of Tops Friendly Market's powdered doughnuts beside it, their second. No other mistakes followed. Now, as the sober thoughts pour in, she remembers she'll need to change her tampon soon and begin to think about what to say to her boyfriend.

READER

Caucasian female, early 50s, with short-cropped
salt-and-pepper hair, wearing a navy blue wharf coat,
collar upturned, faded jeans, hiking boots,
and a silver ring on her right pinky.

=

The Selected Stories of Patricia Highsmith
Patricia Highsmith
(Norton, 2001)
about three quarters through

=

A Quick Peek

She undoes her passenger seat belt to fumble with the buttons of her sweater top. "Slow down a bit; I'm not ready."

Every Christmas morning, she and the Wednesday night bingo caller at the community centre, her best friend since high school, pack a cooler of champagne and orange juice and hit the highways looking for lonely truckers. They take turns — driver and passenger. While one pulls up beside a rig, the other rolls down the window to flash her naked breasts. If the guy isn't a creep, and they are drunk enough, they let him finish off. Otherwise, it's a quick peek and a perky smile, before they roar ahead to the next rig.

She adjusts the satin scarf around her neck, an early gift from her boyfriend, tightening the knot, packaging herself to look like a stewardess.

"Okay, make this one fast," she says. "I gotta put the turkey in the oven."

The bingo caller bursts into schoolgirl giggles and leans on the horn.

READER

Caucasian female, early 50s, with short blond hair,
wearing red fleece jacket, dark blue jeans,
and bright white sneakers.

Bel Canto
Ann Patchett
(HarperCollins, 2005)
P 22

One Boy In

The tranquility of his morning coffee fractured by peeling squeals, neighbourhood kids roughhousing too far out on the ice without their parents' knowledge. He doesn't have kids, doesn't want them. Would serve them right, he thinks, scratching behind his ear while the bread browns in the toaster. Just enough to scare them, he thinks. The clock chimes, the Black-Capped Chickadee announcing 10:00 a.m. The toast is stuck. He tries to free it with the nail of his index finger. The squeals outside reach near mania and he jumps, burnt. Lunging out to the back porch, he scans the lake, pulling his robe tight to his body one moment, throwing it off the next. Sprinting in slippers over frozen goose shit. One boy in, two on the edges.

READER

Caucasian male, late 30s, with short black hair
and goatee, wearing blue bomber jacket, unzipped,
hat in lap, sitting by the window.

King Leary
Paul Quarrington
(Anchor Books, 2007)
P 133

Dress Rehearsal

It's not hard to imagine the drop from their second floor bedroom window. She's played it out nightly, confident she can kick out the screen in time to shimmy onto the ledge and down to safety, a sprained ankle the worst she'd suffer. And what's a sprained ankle? That's why she arranged for their baby girl to stay at her grandmother's for the night, why she bought an extra pack of Marlboros just in case he finished his own and there wasn't anything left to leave lit on the sofa cushion after he'd fallen asleep and she'd gone up to bed.

READER

Caucasian female, late 20s, with powder-pale complexion and long, brown hair, with pink-and-green stripes down each side, wearing worn leather coat and black boots.

The Glass Castle
Jeannette Walls
(Scribner, 2006)
P 32

(In)digestion

As they prepared the next day's lunches, it was her son's job to cut the fruit and veggies. It was the only way he'd eat them. She would just as soon throw a whole apple and carrot into his bag. But he couldn't have anything left over, anything that would require scraping a plate, tossing a core, or shedding a peel. He would only digest that which completely disappeared. He didn't eat food so much as hoard it. As a young child, this required many lectures detailing the significant difference between a grape and a pebble. Or, shelled nuts and a ball of Silly Putty still pressed inside a toy capsule from the shopping mall vending machine.

READER

Black female, late 30s, with short spiky hair
and thin arched eyebrows, wearing red trench coat,
white dress pants, and open-toed sandals.
An open lunch bag sits zipped open in her lap,
full of containers of cubed fruit and carrot sticks.

Middlesex
Jeffrey Eugenides
(Knopf, 2003)
P 205

Legal Limits

She couldn't yet bait her own hook, but she was able to set it, slowing reeling in the pickerel, her first-ever catch. She butted the rod's handle against her hip as the guide reached out a long arm, steadying himself against the side. No net, no net, he whispered, pinching the line and swinging the fish in to his chest. He scanned the water for other vessels, then relaxed, the promise of celebratory breakfast beer confirmed by his wide grin. He patted her shoulder. She'd done good. Real good.

She adjusted her cap and leaned back into the sun, her eyes watering against the glare of a bright morning sky. The sharp crack startled her. She turned to see the guide's hands tight around the fish's head, a flutter of bright pink fanned out over the bottom of the boat.

READER

Asian female, mid-20s, with short blond hair,
wearing thick eyeliner, tight blue jeans,
long green sweater, and white flip flops.

The Time in Between
David Bergen
(McClelland & Stewart, 2005)
P 139

He Didn't See It Coming

The fight was long done, though the dinner plates were still sitting on the kitchen table. They lay beside one another in bed staring at the ceiling, neither wanting to be the first to roll over. She could hear his eyelids clicking. He was looking for clues, filing back through the moments he might have known the fight was about to begin. They'd argued about her hair. She'd cut it all off wanting to look like Mia Farrow in *Rosemary's Baby*. He'd said he liked it, very much, and he did. He'd meant it. But she'd said there was one patch of hair growing out differently. He hadn't noticed. He thought it looked fine, he'd said. He loved her eyes, they were surely the highlight of her head, he'd wanted to add, but he'd waited too long and she'd started yelling, "It's like you can't even see me!" Didn't he see, she'd continued, that suddenly she realized she couldn't trust him to save her in time. In time for what, he'd asked. "I mean, what if a car was coming?" she'd spat. He'd stammered. A car? She hated it when he stammered. He hated it when she'd had too much wine, but he listened, hopeful she would make sense soon. She'd pushed her chair from the kitchen table, abandoning him and their untouched meals. "My point," she'd concluded, steadying herself against the bannister on her way up to their bedroom, "is that you think it's just hair. But one day it will be the speed of an approaching car that you don't notice. You'll be the last thing I see. And it will be all your fault."

READER

Black female, late 30s, with long hair,
wearing white hoodie under black jacket
and tan leather boots.

═════

Isobel and Emile
Alan Reed
(Coach House Books, 2010)
P 78

═════

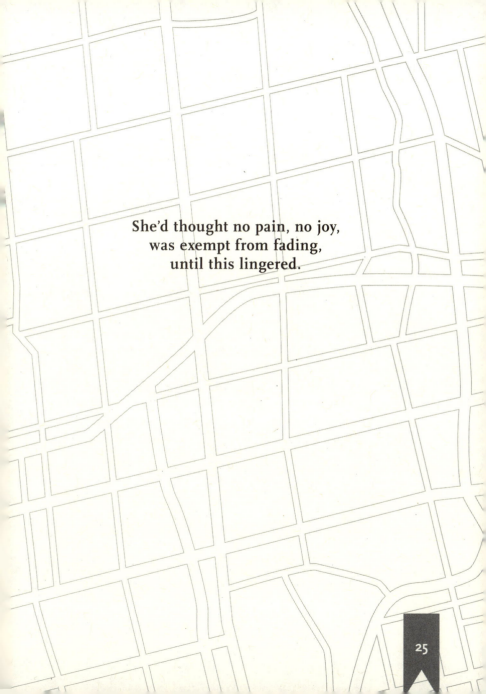

She'd thought no pain, no joy,
was exempt from fading,
until this lingered.

Breaking Ties

The lace on his left shoe has snapped. He resents the caution he needs to observe each morning, to tie a crude knot, the monkey in the middle between two rusted eyelets. What was once an act of physical memory — really, he thinks, when was the last time I remember putting on my shoes? — has become as bothersome as the realization that school won't end any time soon. He prolongs taking his shoes off at night, stubbornly carting a dried leaf from the curb through his living room and into the bedroom, its dusty skeleton, laid to rest, beside the shoe rack.

READER

East African male, mid-20s, wearing black leather jacket, black cap, red glasses, and slick lip gloss.

=====

The Retreat
David Bergen
(McClelland & Stewart, 2008)
halfway through

=====

Six Spin

He remembers running up to the Six Spin at the fairground. When he got to the entrance, he froze at the sight of the girl taking tickets. He recognized her from football games, where she sat on the other end of the bleachers, reading by the field lights.

Brigitte — the name he'd given her — was tall for a girl, at least six feet. She wore the requisite carnival uniform, blue polo shirt, and cream-coloured shorts. But, while other attendants wore white sneakers with tennis socks, she wore high-laced black boots with steel toes. Her commitment to the park-regulated blue baseball cap was half-assed, at best, the hat sitting on the edge of her razor-cut black bob.

He hiked up his big brother's hand-me-down jeans, staring up into Brigitte's face as he handed her his tickets, enamoured with the thick makeup outlining her eyes, curving up to her temples. In place of hoop earrings, she wore safety pins; one ear's ragged hole was infected.

She was, in a word, stunning. She was a girl he could want to be.

READER

Caucasian male, early 40s, short and stalky,
with bright blue eyes, wearing grey jacket,
black scarf, and green cargo pants.

By Grand Central Station I Sat Down and Wept
Elizabeth Smart
(HarperCollins, 1991)
P 41

Morning Glories

He slips out, leaving his lover asleep, and makes his way down the hill to the bay. He sits on the steps, pulls his hoodie over his head to shade his eyes from the glare off the water. A radio plays somewhere down the channel, a sample of early '80s soft rock. He slips off his shorts and hoodie, shielding his penis from the breeze. He inches a step lower and dangles the fingers of his free hand into the water. A spider waxes the surface. He holds himself safe, eyeing a stripped birch branch bobbing against the shoreline, and indulges in a lazy tug set back from view before gliding into the water for the first of twenty laps.

READER

Black male, late 40s, wearing dark suit, striped tie, and leather shoes, carrying Roots backpack with compass key chain.

A Blind Man Can See How Much I Love You
Amy Bloom
(Random House, 2000)
P 50

House Rules

She settles into his chest, the bathwater rising around her collarbone. He strokes her arms, her thighs, reaches below the water and rests his fingers on her hips, tapping. It's her decision. She rolls over, rests her breasts against him, kissing his neck below the scar. He wraps his arms around her, satisfied with her gesture. They'll make it another day.

READER

Caucasian female, early 40s, with short strawberry blond hair, wearing simple silver stud in left nostril, long green coat, and crushed velvet scarf, carrying teal umbrella.

Not That Kind of Girl
Catherine Alliott
(Headline Book Publishing, 2005)
p 166

Complementary Colours

In grad school, he saw a film he didn't understand. The girl who made it was shy and pretty and always sat in the front row. The film was quiet and blue. Everything so blue. From the bathwater, to the kitchen kettle, to the drapes softly suckled by the slightly open mouth of a screenless window.

When the horse appeared out of the fog, it too was blue. As it lumbered closer to the camera, he'd begun to cry, the horse's last laboured breaths indistinguishable from the cloud cover.

She'd turned in her chair to look back at the boy awash in blue, the boy in the orange shirt.

READER

Caucasian male, mid-50s, with scruffy white hair,
wearing glasses, tan pants, burgundy sweater,
and brown leather boots.

Blood Meridian
Cormac McCarthy
(Vintage, 1992)
P 117

Surplus

She buys the jacket across the border at an army surplus store. She talks the owner down to twenty bucks. It's heavy brown suede, each of its cuffs worn into a smooth crease from years of rolling. It zips flat up the front, to the middle of her ribs, but not over her chest. It's a man's jacket, after all. She adjusts the collar, snapping it high, even though it falls limp almost immediately.

It comes with a receipt in the breast pocket: five bucks of gasoline from a station one town over, and a tissue crumpled over a chewed-up piece of gum in a Big Red wrapper and the filter of a Marlboro. A day's worth of sour breath, left to curdle second-hand.

READER

Caucasian female, early 30s, wearing black jeans, black-and-white sneakers, worn brown suede jacket, and headphones, carrying orange courier bag.

Prozac Nation
Elizabeth Wurtzel
(Houghton Mifflin, 1994)
P 101

Small Talks

She stands outside the apartment, half-drained bottle concealed inside a knotted plastic bag, the result of a sidebar session in the subway washroom after she received the text saying that he'd be at the party. Talking. Talking about politics. Talking about war. Talking about things that matter to her. Things she promised herself she wouldn't talk about anymore at parties because she becomes That Girl. The one who talks about politics at parties. The one who reacts to what you say.

READER

Asian female, early 20s, wearing blue-and-red knitted cap, jean jacket under black vest, and jeans rolled high over black biker boots.

Ticknor
Sheila Heti
(House of Anansi Press, 2005)
p 65

Lots and Lots

There are only twenty-six underground parking spaces in her three-storey building. She's occupied #18 since 1997. He's had #20 since 2003. #19 became vacant in 2005, left free for visitors if they reserved ahead of time. Seeing one another through the empty space, they rarely say a thing. Occasionally they lift their travel mugs to one another to greet the day, or pause long enough to wonder aloud in unison if the superintendent will ever get around to fixing the faulty door on the shared washing machine. This weekend, #19 wasn't empty. Out of province plates. Soft leather briefcase in back. Diet cola can in the cup holder. Monday morning, the car was gone, an oil stain marking the centre of #19, the diet cola can sitting under the No Smoking sign, ashes flecked around the tab. They peered at one another through the gap between their spaces, got into their cars, and checked their mirrors for oncoming traffic.

READER

South Asian female, mid-50s, with curly
shoulder-length hair pulled back in loose ponytail,
wearing fine gold-rimmed glasses and black jacket.

Feels Like Family
Sherryl Woods
(Mira, 2010)
P 113

Woman and Parrot

Her grandmother's Chrysler Imperial rumbled down the road away from the farm and into the city for supplies, leaving her, 12 years old, with a squawking parrot and a nearly blind woman scanning the excessively large print of Thomas Hardy's *Far from the Madding Crowd*. No pages to turn, she curled her shoulders forward, biting her nails, and clearing her throat to punctuate the silence, reminding the woman she was still in the room. She focused on the woman's fingernails, soft pink and peeling like discarded clam shells. The parrot called for dinner. "Oh, balls," the woman proclaimed, pushing herself back from the table, startled by the sudden surprise of a young stranger beside her.

READER

Asian female, 30s, with long brown hair under white knit cap, wearing blue peacoat and jeans tucked into white leather boots.

The Book of Negroes
Lawrence Hill
(HarperCollins, 2007)
p 87

Dreams of a Would-Be Government Employee

When had she abandoned her dream to become a rural mail carrier, to drive on the shoulder, to back up against the flow of traffic like a clown car in a Shriners' Parade, to shower each package's recipient with a handful of wrapped candy?

READER

Caucasian female, mid-20s, with blond hair
clipped up, wearing red peacoat,
white leather purse, and grey UGGS.

———

Total Control
David Baldacci
(Grand Central Publishing, 1997)
P 130

———

Simple Sandwiches

For the third night in a row, he'd dreamt of his colleague. In the dreams, they never touch. They don't kiss. You couldn't even really say they hugged. They lean against one another in the break room while they eat their simple cheese and lettuce sandwiches, breast to breast, chin to shoulder, delighting in the explicit domesticity of their inferred affair.

READER

Caucasian male, 50s, with silver hair and jet-black eyebrows, wearing long wool coat and wraparound earmuffs.

Mordecai, The Life & Times
Charles Foran
(Knopf, 2010)
P 41

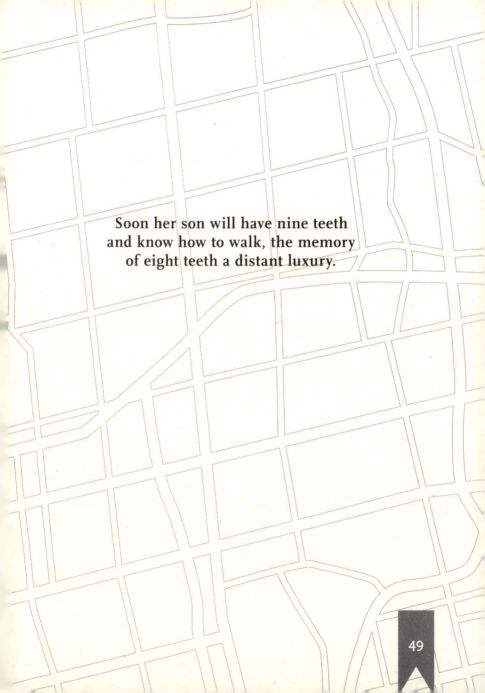

Soon her son will have nine teeth
and know how to walk, the memory
of eight teeth a distant luxury.

Tho. Shelton

From his hospice bed, he stares at the framed 1819 aqua tint of the boxer Tho. Shelton, brought by his son from home. Shelton stands at the ready, fists raised and loosely clenched, razored bangs combed forward into a handsome peak, pencil-thin sideburns tracing the line of his square jaw. But it's the bloated belly below the tie of the boxer's pants he's taken with, and the way the boxer's frame leans like an expectant mother, hips jutting forward. A grandchild, he thinks, how wonderful, and rests the phone back in its cradle.

READER

Caucasian male, with short brown hair,
wearing blue tuque, green scarf, and
red-and-white striped second-hand sweater.

Spook: Science Tackles the Afterlife
Mary Roach
(Norton, 2005)
P 79

Bagged Lunch

This morning, he woke up on the edge of pleasure, the taste of foil hitting the back of his tongue, double chocolate licked from the wrapper of a pudding cup. His lunch bag holds the remnants of last night's dinner, a rushed mash of canned peas, boiled potatoes, and breaded chicken thigh. But for today's lunch he'll have to go without dessert.

READER

Caucasian boy, 11–12 years old, with soft brown curly hair, wearing faded blue cable-knit sweater stretched about the shoulders and waist.

One Beastly Beast
Garth Nix, illustrated by Brian Biggs
(HarperCollins, 2007)
P 35

Miss Popular

Watching her reflection in the television screen, she practices smoking, leaning heavy into the couch cushion. Her friends look silly when they try to light a cigarette, wincing as if on *Fear Factor* and asked to chew through a hundred-year-old egg. She doesn't see the point if you're not going to enjoy it. Which is not to say that she does. She's looking for things to be remembered for after they've graduated, gotten soft, and had three children with men they met at their first jobs. As if, twenty years from now, they'll gather for a girls' weekend and the prettiest of them will note the curl of smoke escaping her lips, washing over her tongue like mist, and sigh, "You always were the cool one. And you haven't changed a bit."

READER

South Asian female, early 20s, with short brown bob, wearing white wool sweater underneath open blue peacoat, three charms hanging from a long golden chain around her neck.

Herzog
Saul Bellow
(Penguin, 2003)
P 105

Riding the Rails

He's a young boy, about ten, moving his tray along the rails, considering the desserts. JELL-O, red and green cubes, in a glass sundae dish, topped with a hardening dollop of piped whipped cream. Milk chocolate pudding in a glass dish, topped, again, with a hardening dollop of piped whipped cream. A glass bowl of creamy rice pudding with raisins. Something layered and spongy with a dusting of chocolate slivers. He lifts it and smells. Alcohol.

A cuckoo clock strikes the hour and he turns to scan the dark wood-panelled wall. A bird slides in and out of the clock with each chime, while a lederhosened couple chase each other around its base.

He looks toward the long hall leading to the women's washroom, back to his table and his grandmother's beige purse, tan overcoat. She has trouble swallowing, and she's been gone a long time.

READER

Caucasian male, early 40s, settled deep
into easy chair, legs crossed at the ankle.

The Communist's Daughter
Dennis Bock
(HarperCollins, 2007)
P 177

It Begins the Same

He's a boy again, riding his bike, its wheels threaded with raw meat. The dog soon catches up and nips at his heels, drool wagging from its jaw. He pedals faster and loses his footing, the flesh of his ankle peels back to resemble the soft interior of the dog's mouth. He pushes his heel to the dog's forehead until it whimpers into submission. He rides off. When he looks down again, the dog's teeth chatter loose the spokes, some studding in his calf, trailing red ribbons.

READER

Caucasian male, wearing black knitted cap with
Canadian crest, Sony headphones, brown cords,
green plaid dress shirt, and black West Beach jacket.

———

Slaughterhouse-Five
Kurt Vonnegut
(Dial Press Trade Paperback, 1999)
P 48

———

Pillow Talk

Her husband surprised her last night. It was bright and soft, friendly and forgiving, and placed beside the toilet in time for her next treatment.

She rested her cheek against his forehead and held him as he wept.

READER

Black female, early 30s, with shaved head and pencilled-in eyebrows, wearing all black, carrying black-and-hot-pink backpack, black-and-hot-pink padlock attached to zipper.

———

Town House
Tish Cohen
(HarperCollins, 2007)
near the beginning

———

The Health Hustle

He waits his turn in a line of young boys doing somersaults along a blue runway pad. Crouching and tucking. Standing, and crouching, and tucking. That's what's evaluated in Grade Six Phys. Ed., the graceful execution of a tuck and roll, or the ability to scale a rope to the top knot or hold a chin-up for at least a minute all indications of his well-rounded potential. Watching the girls lunge toward the pummel horse, which of us, he wonders, will sprout the first pit hair, get to second base, or deal the sting of a dodge ball against a girl's tender thighs? He approaches the pad, rolls over his shoulder, called out by his teacher for an incomplete somersault.

The music starts — "Pop Corn"— and the girls and boys form rows and mirror the disco-timed exercises of his teacher, his uncanny sense of rhythm lost on everyone in the gymnasium.

READER

Caucasian male, late 30s, with short brown hair,
wearing glasses and blue-and-pink striped shirt,
carrying folded-over black plastic bag under his arm.

No One Belongs Here More Than You
Miranda July
(Scribner, 2008)
P 91

Swedish Berries

The girl stayed on the hotel beach reading, peering up from her book to see if her mother was still talking to that man. They stood in the surf, his nipples breaking out of his white chest hair, thick and red, like Swedish berries, once her favourite snack. The man took the tips of her mother's fingers while she lowered herself onto her belly and he floated her back and forth, offering constant reminders to kick and breathe, chin up and breathe. Then more insistent: chin up and breathe.

When the girl looked up next, the man was sitting on the beach, clutching his foot, toes fanned like frill-necked lizard. Her mother stayed in the surf, each passing wave urging her toward shore. But the girl could see what her mother saw, that this man got too angry too fast. They'd dine alone that night. Whatever the girl wanted, she could have.

READER

Asian female, early 30s, with short brown hair, wearing
glasses, grey jacket, blue collared shirt,
and dark blue jeans.

———

The Origin of Species
Nino Ricci
(Doubleday, 2008)
P 251

———

Mercy

He'd never so much as buried a pet. He left the flushing of goldfish to his wife. The smell of earth alone after a hard rain turned his stomach.

When the crate arrived, an East Coast delivery of lobster on ice, the note tucked inside the birthday card contained pencil sketches to help him through the process. His brother was a different sort, brave or careless. He wasn't sure which. He would follow the instructions if only because more than killing a creature he hated ignoring a gift. He held the lobster at arm's length, stroking its head as per the illustration, the lobster's body falling limp within moments, completely at his mercy, harmless. Afraid that it was all too easy — was it all this easy? — he threw the lobster back on ice determined never to go down that dark path again.

READER

Caucasian male, mid-40s, with short brown hair,
wearing charcoal-grey suit under open blue parka.

———

Crime and Punishment
Fyodor Dostoevsky
(Dover, 2001)
about one quarter in

———

Clearcutting

That morning, her mother had opened her eyes long enough to squint. She pointed a frail finger at the blinds beside her hospital bed. The lines, she said, were cutting the sky. Would someone please erase the lines so she could see it all?

READER

Caucasian female, 50s, with ruffled blond hair, wearing heavy winter coat, Baffin winter boots, carrying a bright floral purse.

Wuthering Heights
Emily Bronte
(Dover, 1996)
P 145

What had their love been
if not the exception?

Love Noted

When she gets to page three, she'll find a confession of love scribbled in the margin. Her heart will leap, even though she knows it wasn't written by the man who gifted her the book; it was bought secondhand. It's not his handwriting, but she'll give in to the hope, just the same, because people don't use words like those anymore, and how lovely would it be to imagine that he could be somewhere imagining her, standing on the subway platform, bouncing on the balls of her feet, having just turned to page three.

READER

Caucasian female, late 20s, with long brown hair tied back in a neat ponytail, wearing purple broad-framed glasses, a long red wool coat, and a green-and-red flecked angora scarf. She uses a gift tag as her bookmark.

=

The Whole Story and other stories
Ali Smith
(Hamish Hamilton, 2003)
P 1

=

Ends

After dinner, they sat at opposite ends of the couch, reading, and rubbing each other's calves. He held a fist to his mouth. Must have been something he ate, he apologized. No, he couldn't control it, he said, stretching out, the bottom of his T-shirt rising to reveal his belly button breaking into a hairy grin. She stared at it for ages, clenching and releasing her abdomen. Did he not feel that? That nakedness? She glared at the spot on his forehead where the creases had begun to tunnel into his eyebrows, the patch of sun-worn skin on his upper left cheek, that stubborn grey in his beard.

She looked down at her legs, the ridges on her yellowing toe nails, a curl of purple veins circling the inside of her knee, and put the book down.

When had this happened?

READER

Caucasian female, late 30s, with strawberry-blond hair,
wearing brown skirt and lime-green blouse
with sleeves rolled and buttoned at the elbow.
Sunglasses sit in lap.

———

The Kite Runner
Khaled Hosseini
(Anchor Canada, 2004)
P 157

———

The Young Lovers, Part I

She wears her pistachio-green overcoat. White pants out of season. He sports a crop of red blemishes on his chin. They teeter an arm's length apart, their heads within inches of one another. She carefully words a sentence he's struggling to catch. She mouths it three times, four. The edges of his lips curl and she realizes he knows perfectly well what she's saying. She cuffs his arm with the back of her hand.

"Christmas is coming."

"Christmas is coming."

"Christmas is coming."

"Christmas is — you idiot!"

He smiles that half-smile, something he once saw in a film. He really will turn out to be a sexy and attentive man, a purposefully sexy and attentive man. His smile draws in others and he's suddenly self-conscious when adult women, rosy in the cheeks, catch themselves staring and turn away.

She continues, "This Saturday? We'll do it this Saturday?"

It's possible they'll go shopping, where their hands will most certainly brush in the Saturday crush of holiday shoppers. They'll share food court poutine, he'll offer to carry her bag from the Disney Store, and they'll stand face-to-face on the escalator, their first kiss floating toward ground level.

READER

Caucasian girl, 16–17...

———

Cerebus #300
Dave Sim, illustrated by Gerhard
(Aardvark-Vanaheim, 2004)
P 12

———

The Young Lovers, Part II

Crammed together in the doorway of the subway, she looks paler than usual, her blue eyes popping neon. He struggles to toe the cuffs of his ski pants over the top of his boots, circling his shoulders, bundled too tightly inside his winter gear, as a bead of sweat threatens to extend its path below the nape of his neck to his shoulder blade. A wet mop of curls itches under his tuque. He flexes his ears, bobs his brow, anything to get relief. She finally traces a finger over his forehead, tucking a strand of hair under the rim. He feels her touch clear through to his belly.

He shuffles his weight as the subway curves, rocking between her and the passenger wedged behind him, a gentleman pressed sharp from head to toe, his cologne crisp and clean, the pointed tip of his black dress shoes extending inches past any shoe the boy has ever seen. This man has no need for a jacket. He might even live in one of those posh hotels, one of those posh people who never need to go outside, a posh rat. The boy smiles sweetly at him, when the subway comes to a sudden stop halfway through the tunnel. The man lurches forward, placing the pads of his fingers against the boy's lower spine. Stunned, the boy turns to confront him. And then the soft, forgiving smile as he takes in that there is something otherworldly about the man, before turning back to face his girlfriend.

READER

... with long brown hair and Husky-blue eyes,
wearing pistachio-green spring coat (out of season),
brown corduroy pants, and red sneakers.

―――

The Truth About Forever
Sarah Dessen
(Penguin, 2006)
P 1

―――

Biopsy

The night before his girlfriend's biopsy, they decided to get serious about their health. They sat on the bed and he drew a line down the centre of the page. "Okay," he said, nodding as if psyching himself up for some athletic feat. "I propose we divide the list into two columns." His hand shook as he wrote out the headings. "Things We Keep," he recited aloud. "That would be the good habits. And Things We Cut Off." It would continue to dawn on him for an agonizingly long time just how remarkable a slip it was.

READER

Asian male, mid-20s, with short brown hair,
wearing broad-framed glasses, pink collared shirt
under brown cardigan, and purple paisley scarf.

Choke
Chuck Palahniuk
(Anchor, 2002)
P 43

Cherry

On her first date with the bouncer she'd worn a plastic cherry necklace, telling him it was crystal. He'd laughed and pulled her closer, his stubble stinging her chin. "Women twice your age come into the bar every night. Women with jobs and cars. But I could learn to love a girl like you. You have class," he'd whispered, her first kiss with a man on full display in a mall food court. She wondered if Cherry Chapstick could be a real name, imagining a time when the bouncer might actually own the bar and she could go in any night of the week and drink for free and be called to the stage to share a song.

READER

Caucasian female, late 30s, with short brown hair,
wearing blue striped sweater under
black winter jacket.

Star Island
Carl Hiaasen
(Knopf, 2010)
P 5

Love Will Tear Us Apart

Their first Christmas together, they held hands in bed and promised that even if one of them ended up in a wheelchair, they'd stay together. If he lost an eyebrow to a grease fire, she'd stay. "And if you lose your hearing to a cotton swab, I'll stay," he'd added. They laughed and pressed their foreheads close, folding their gaze into shallow focus, knowing full well that no one knows why or when they'll leave, that even joy can tear two people apart.

READER

Caucasian female, 40s, with long brown hair wearing bright red lipstick, black-and-white polka-dot dress and carrying a matching bag.

How Doctors Think
Jerome Groopman
(Houghton Mifflin Harcourt, 2008)
P 101

Divorced Before Thirty

He's kept his job longer than his marriage. It really hadn't been that big of a thing, he'd thought, but it was big to him. He'd simply asked her to leave the washroom. (He never liked to fight while he was naked.) Then there was the click of the front door closing and the sound of her heels on the hall tile toward the elevator. Had she even locked the door? He'd rushed from the bathroom to the apartment door, his wet feet sinking into the shallow carpet. He peered through the door peephole, her shape obscured by the wide lens. Were they done talking? He strained to keep her in view. At the elevator, she'd adjusted her purse strap and rubbed her forehead. Was she crying, he'd wondered? No, no, darling. He ran his fingers through his hair and turned the doorknob just as the elevator chimed. Stepping out into the hallway, clothed in nothing but a towel, he saw her smiling, laughing even, as a neighbour's hand reached out to hold the elevator door open. Fine, thank you, she'd said. *Great,* actually.

READER

Caucasian male, late 20s, with short black hair
and beard, wearing black fleece, grey tuque,
grey cords, and Sorels.

Half of a Yellow Sun
Chimamanda Ngozi Adichie
(Vintage, 2007)
P 306

Flat

The cat has commandeered the empty boxes and the bathroom window ledge, the only window in the basement bachelor. The bath fills while she admires the clean interior of the fridge. A lone bottle of beer sits in the crisper. Would the last tenant come back to claim it? Was it a housewarming gift? She decides for the both of them, twists off the top, and takes a long haul, opening the oven to preheat the apartment.

Four mirror squares on the south wall extend the flat.

She dips a foot into the bathwater, running her toe over a chip in the basin that's begun to rust, then submerges her calf, winter's growth standing on edge. The cat jaws his way through a piece of kibble, the only familiar sound in this new home. She sinks into the tub completely, places the beer on the floor beside her, and releases her ample belly. For how long, she wonders, has she been holding this in?

READER

Caucasian female, late 20s, with short, reddish hair, wearing pale green turtleneck sweater under white winter jacket.

The Beauty of Humanity Movement
Camilla Gibb
(Doubleday Canada, 2010)
P 122

Side Tables

Her side table holds her lemon cuticle cream, a packet of tissue, an eyeglasses case, and a bottle of Aspirin. His side table holds a nail clipper, a packet of tissue, an eyeglasses case, and an emptied glass of Scotch.

Her book is in her lap, traded instead for a journal and pen to write with, a quick scribble to jog the memory tomorrow. His book is a collection of jumbo crosswords, resting on his chest. His head back, eyes closed.

Her feet are elevated, ankles swollen and aching. His feet peek out beyond the comforter, his long frame never having spent a night entirely on their marriage mattress.

Her breath is steady, pleasantly winding down. His breath has stopped.

Her kiss on his forehead.

Her body rolling away.

Her hand reaching for his.

READER

Caucasian female, 60ish, with white hair, wearing square glasses, beige jacket, and purple scarf.

Close Case
Alafair Burke
(St. Martin's Press, 2006)
P 254

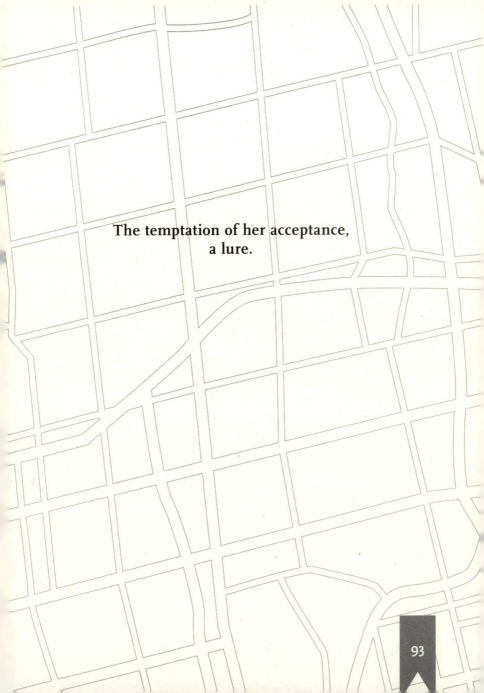

The temptation of her acceptance,
a lure.

Sticks and Twigs

The man beside her on the streetcar wears a long buckskin jacket with fringes lining its hem, the backs of his arms. He's in his late 50s, face worn, a shock of spiky, bleached blond hair growing out at the roots. He hunches over his cupped hand, pinching marijuana sticks and twigs into as fine a powder as possible. He looks up at each stop, squinting at each passerby, then going back to the task at hand.

Another man boards and stands over him. His skin is baby smooth, tanned. He wears a pressed shirt under a high-collared, half-zipped, Jacquard pullover. His tweed cap is jaunty and cocked to one side. He considers his reflection, bumping the elbow of the man in the buckskin jacket who yells, "Hey, Buddy! I don't got all the room in the world!"

The dapper man kneels down to eye level and speaks in a low voice. "Hey, brother. I didn't mean to get in your space. We good, friend?"

The man in the buckskin jacket presses his knees together and shelters his stash, turning his weight toward the woman reading beside him. "Yeah, man," he mumbles back. "We're good. I just don't got all the room in the world."

READER

Caucasian female, late 40s, with short brown hair,
wearing black coat, dark violet scarf,
and black leather gloves.

———

Payback
Margaret Atwood
(House of Anansi Press, 2008)
P 42

———

Intrusion

He was thirteen years old, stretched out on the carpet in the basement, watching television before bed. The windows were propped open, screens in place to deter the neighbour's curious dog from poking in her head. The sound of feet passing by didn't startle him. All outside noises had become one — ball hockey, wrestling cats, a car radio. The gate was locked. If someone was in the backyard, it would mean they'd scaled the fence.

That was the night he learned to believe in monsters.

READER

East African male, mid-30s, wearing brown leather jacket, white dress shirt, purple bow tie, and tweed cap.

———

World War Z: An Oral History of the Zombie War
Max Brooks
(Three Rivers Press, 2007)
about halfway in

———

Simmer

She stands in front of the pot, stirring through the bubbles, the room lit only by the dim yellow stove light. Steam rises in her face. She rests her hand on the stovetop and finds it warm to the touch. It calms her. She turns down the burner heat and lets the stew simmer, scratching her ankle with the heel of her piggy slipper. She draws in a deep breath and exhales loudly, plunging her hands into the pockets of her fleece housecoat. The stew settles into a steady roil, peppers, onions, and carrots turning up over thick chunks of cubed beef. She pulls the Bisquick from the cupboard, ripping open the top, giggling as the dry mix puffs up in her face.

She doesn't feel like cleaning tonight.

There is so much food to share. It's a shame he won't be here to taste it.

Oh, but if she doesn't clean tonight she'll dread the coming day.

She puts the lid on the stew and turns the heat right down, heading into the bathroom with gloves and garbage bags, the tub filled with stripped bones.

READER

Caucasian female, late 40s, wearing puffy jacket with hood and powder-blue hand-knitted cap. Her book is covered in a bright green fabric jacket, patterned with gift boxes and red stars.

Misery
Stephen King
(Signet, 2010)
P 107

Cursive

She's sitting in her wicker chair in the sunroom, looking at the ravine outside her window, wondering if the rabbits have been digging in her garden. She pads her thumb over the cheese tray, picking up the last of the Melba toast, leaving nothing to waste, and finishes her port. She thinks about the children. Quiet down now, she imagines. Eyes front for the national anthem. She bumped into one the other day, married and with such good posture. Remarkable. Did she know she'd been her favourite teacher, the woman had asked. Can you imagine? After all this time. A favourite? Still, she'd struggled to recall, settling on a memory that could have been any number of students. There were so many, after all, and not one sick day. But, yes, she'd responded. Thank you. Of course, she remembered her. Such a bright child. A happy child. And she'd grown into a beautiful woman. Just like her daughter, she'd have to imagine.

READER

Caucasian male, mid-50s, wearing burgundy T-shirt,
grey shorts, and sandals.

═

Harry Potter and the Deathly Hallows
J.K. Rowling
(Raincoast, 2007)
P 186

═

Winter Wonderland

The sight of the baby squirrel frozen inches beneath the iced-over surface under the cottage's drain pipe was enough to scare her. She chipped around it, her pants pocket full of seeds, an offering to the grouse she'd come to call Pet. The squirrel's eyes were haunting, loose and broken, like those of an old porcelain doll.

When the grouse flew up in her face, she instinctively swung the spade, batting the bird to the base of the nearest birch. It hissed and spread its wings when she tried to get closer, striking at her wrist when she palmed a pile of seed at its feet.

She felt her finger twitch against the spade. Resting it against a neighbouring tree, she backed toward the cottage to resist temptation. She didn't trust nature. But she'd give the grouse five minutes to get out of there.

READER

East Indian female, mid-20s, wearing skinny jeans, jean jacket with hoodie, and light scarf.

Mean Boy
Lynn Coady
(Anchor Canada, 2006)
P 20

Indiana Summers

In the eighth grade, she became best friends with a boy whose father owned the carpet store in town. They had three cars. One was an orange Corvette that sat on blocks in the garage until his sixteenth birthday. His family owned a big house with a huge lot, close to the canal.

The summer after grade eight, she learned how to crack a whip like Indiana Jones and pump up an air gun to shoot the necks off discarded vodka bottles.

One afternoon, they'd come running out of the brush — Pow! Pow! Pow! — and only then saw the line of cars parked alongside the neighbouring cemetery. A row of heads above dark suits looked up. She lowered her gun, her friend snickering, his blackened big toe poking a hole through the tip of his Converse sneaker. Passing the open grave, she flinched, shooting herself in the ankle while paying her respects. The boy would swear she pulled the trigger on purpose.

READER

Caucasian female, mid-20s, blond hair pulled back in neat, freshly washed ponytail, wearing white leather jacket, purple scarf, and purple heels.

Three Day Road
Joseph Boyden
(Penguin Canada, 2008)
P 118

Pinhead

He stands in the doorway of a hair salon holding a bag from La Vie en Rose. He stares out into the street making strained eye contact with random pedestrians like a hostage in a bank robbery. They return his gaze as if to say, What's keeping you? Whitney Houston's *Greatest Hits* are in rotation with The Scissor Sisters, the *Sliver* soundtrack, Bette Midler, and Gino Vinnelli. Men in tight T-shirts, some of them with pierced nipples, he can see, tend to a salon full of women much like his latest wife, women in their early 30s straddling the line between casual youth and business casual. She's calling to him. Would he come back and sit down already? Her hairdresser repeats the plea, emphasizing his sibilants just to make him uncomfortable. He's older, true, but he's not that guy. He really couldn't care less who the hairdresser's banging. It's his wife's head. When it's wet, it just looks so small.

READER

Native Canadian female, mid-20s, wearing jean jacket with brown turtleneck sweater up over chin, taupe scarf, green cargo pants, and leather shoes with a thick tread.

Baby Proof
Emily Giffin
(St. Martins Press, 2006)
P 115

'86

Out of eleven-thousand applicants, a woman from Concord, New Hampshire would represent them all, the first teacher to be launched into space. At another school, another teacher calls the students over to the portable television cart. The broadcast is about to begin. The teacher gathers her young students closer, her arms folded tight over her chest as they wait for the countdown to begin. From the impossible to the remarkable and then — in a single deafeningly quiet moment — the unimaginable, it is done. A plume of smoke inflates across the sky like a parade balloon. The children squeal. Many of them think it looks like a caterpillar, its antennae reaching out, seeking. The teacher prays that once its folds plump up, its body extended in full, it will unveil something hopeful, a sign of life. Instead, it fades, a bright blue sky all that remains.

READER

Asian male, mid-20s, with neat black hair, wearing fogged glasses, black wharf jacket, and black corduroy cap.

Stiff
Mary Roach
(Norton, 2004)
P 114

Jelly

Her breath is still caught in her chest. She had to run from the streetcar to the office building to escape the rain, her hands too full of Tupperware treats to carry an umbrella. She stamps her feet on the soaked runner, a trickle of foundation tickling her upper lip. She's not in a rush for the elevator, but looks up in time to see her colleague holding her purse in the door. Sure, there's enough room, she says, signaling to "those women," the ones who work a floor above them, who look at her, then each other, to clear a space. To make their point, they inch back against the walls of the elevator, and she knows that one day she'll end up alone with them and they'll tell her to take the stairs, it's not like she couldn't use the exercise. She lunges into a half-spirited jog, the candied smiles of her shortbread snowmen jostled out of place.

READER

Caucasian female, late 30s, wearing large knitted
ski sweater and hat, large leather carryall in lap.

―――

The Pleasure of Finding Things Out:
The Best Short Works of Richard P. Feynman
Richard P. Feynman
(Basic, 2005)
about halfway in

―――

Red

A blizzard blows in the background.

"I'm in the street outside my house," she yells into the phone, "holding a severed leg. I'm guessing a deer. It's a clean cut, only slightly crude. A hunter, I'd say."

"Grand of you to go out in this weather and get it," I say, and settle in for the tale.

"Well, it was just sitting here in the snow. I didn't want a child to come across it." The sound of her blowing into her hands to warm them up. "What?"

"I said, what are you going to do with it?"

"I don't know." Long silence. "How does one dispose of a severed leg?"

"Maybe we should dispose of you."

She enters her house. "Hold on." She's back on the line. "That'll do. It's in the backyard."

"It's ... ?"

"Hold on." It seems she's hung up, but eventually picks up the phone. "OK. All done. I threw it over the fence."

"'Into your neighbour's yard?!"

"No, no. The back fence."

"What's over the fence?"

"A park. *Hold on!*"

READER

Caucasian female, late 30s, with short greying hair, wearing long black coat, red scarf, and glass bauble ring with flower petal floating inside.

═

The Glass Castle
Jeannette Walls
(Scribner, 2006)
P 102

═

Visitor

The single mattress gives in the middle. He picks at a loose button through the fitted sheet and stares at the foot of the bed where his overnight bag sits unpacked. His grandmother's shelves are stacked with travel books, birding guides, poetry, and an old copy of *The Little Prince,* which she'll read to him before bed, as she does every time he comes to visit.

The bedroom window is open a crack. There are no shadows against the drapes but he can hear the branches moving in the breeze, footsteps in the leaves — quiet. Every time he comes to visit.

His heart in his chest, then his throat, now his ears. He remembers Grandma's instructions and readies himself. Tonight, when his eyes shut, the figure will appear silent by his side. But he'll be a big boy and tell that lady she's not welcome in this house anymore. Only when he comes to visit.

READER

Caucasian male, late 20s, with short black hair,
wearing black jeans, white dress shirt,
and grey tweed coat, collar up.

=

Through Black Spruce
Joseph Boyden
(Penguin Canada, 2009)
P 295

=

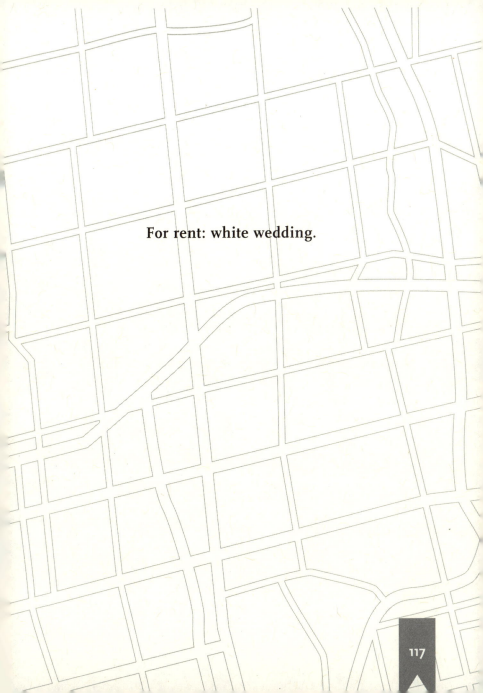

For rent: white wedding.

Irlsgay

When she was ten years old, she sat cross-legged with her best friend inside the midday glow of a blue pup tent and convinced her to play a game, moving the first consonant of a name to its end and tacking on an 'ay' to encode a list of all the girls they'd let kiss them on the mouths, if they had to.

READER

Caucasian female, mid-20s, with long brown hair
tucked into knitted cap.

―――

The City of Words
Alberto Manguel
(House of Anansi Press, 2007)
P 126

―――

A Room of His Own

They've been dating for over a year now, on and off, mostly off, especially if you count the six weeks she travelled abroad, which he does, and they agreed they shouldn't be exclusive not knowing if, or when, they'd take the next step, the next step itself unclear, and even more so because he did stay exclusive, while she didn't, which isn't really even the reason he started to let himself think about this again, it's his writing, and her backyard, which is large and tree-covered and has that little shed that she once suggested way-back-when he could turn into a studio, if they took the next step, but she was at a reading with her friends, and the beer was free, and he didn't know her well enough yet to know if he should believe her, or if he even wanted to look far enough into a future in which he didn't have another girlfriend, or was the guy who didn't fool around in those six weeks, just the guy who wonders what kind of guy he is that he will miss that shed more than her now that he's finally decided.

READER

Caucasian male, late 20s, with long dark hair,
wearing plain white T-shirt, brown cargo shorts,
and black pool sandals.

———

Micro Fiction: An Anthology of Really Short Stories
Edited by Jerome Stern
(Norton, 1996)
about halfway in

———

Sugar Bowls

Four years old, she sat on the edge of the freshly paved tarmac of the townhouse complex in which she lived, on the East Side of town, transferring her lunch, stalks of unwashed rhubarb, back and forth between two large stainless steel bowls, one containing water, the other filled with white sugar, while her brother burned ants through a magnifying glass with a quiet contemplation she'd only seen on their mother's face when cutting coupons.

READER

Caucasian female, late 20s, with long blond hair,
wearing brown hooded sweater, grey scarf,
and black jeans.

=

The Time Machine
H.G. Wells
(Phoenix Pick, 2008)
P 97

=

Esther

His mother's poodle is named after Esther, his great aunt who left the monastery in her 50s to study reproductive medicine.

READER

Caucasian male, mid-30s, with short black hair and stubble, wearing black jeans, black turtleneck, and grey pinstriped suit jacket.

=

The Origin of Species
Nino Ricci
(Doubleday, 2008)
P 1

=

If This Buick Could Talk

His uncle's belongings sit unclaimed in his father's basement: books, mostly, curling in the humidity, a suitcase, its satin pouch stuffed with loose papers, the typewriter it used to contain ribbonless and far away, sitting on the floor of a rusty Buick parked outside a Husky Truck Stop.

READER

South Asian male, late 30s, with curly, shoulder-length black hair, wearing grey dress jacket, black dress shirt, faded jeans, and black leather shoes.

The Book of Secrets
M.G. Vassanji
(McClelland & Stewart, 1994)
P 137

Grace

The minister was the first redhead the boy had ever seen naked, his body hair glowing in the morning sun, shocking the lake's surface, afloat beside the boy's mother, the first woman he'd ever seen naked and swimming with their minister.

READER

Caucasian male, early 50s, with long face, wavy, grey hair parted down the middle, "I Am Salman Rushdie" button pinned on North Face jacket, wearing red jeans and white sneakers.

The God Delusion
Richard Dawkins
(Houghton Mifflin Harcourt, 2008)
P 150

Creature Feature

The longest she'd ever spent in a car was at the drive-in watching a triple creature feature with her immobilized father who waited out a pinched nerve, a watery monster sliding across the screen, while a one-hundred-and-twenty-pound buck sat on ice under the tarp of their hitched trailer.

READER

Caucasian male, late 20s, very tall, wearing blue knit cap, light blue hoodie, and green jacket with red-and-white cross-stitching on the arms.

———

Into the Wild
Jon Krakauer
(Anchor, 1997)
P 174

———

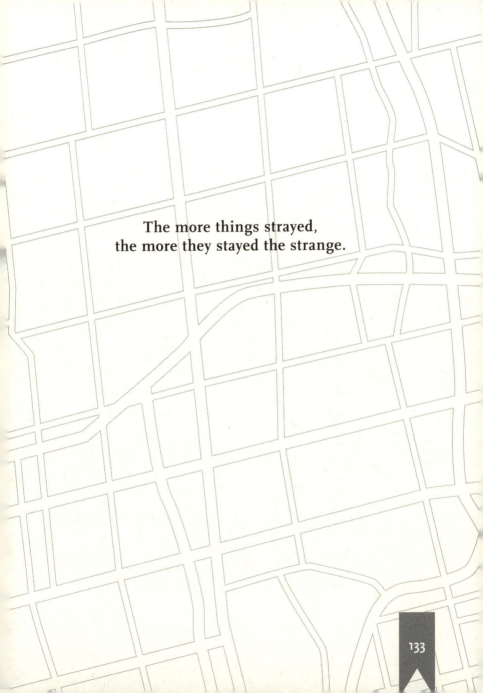

The more things strayed,
the more they stayed the strange.

Girlfriends

She looks forward to the morning commute. She'll ride the subway to the end of the line and take two buses to the warehouse where she'll take her place on the line next to Deb, a lifer married to Brad who's always on the road, and Marlene, a late 40s pre-op transsexual who keeps her hair in a net because it gets frizzy in the humidity.

The snack boxes make their way toward them, the first row already complete: gum, lozenges, and mints. She readies her stock and fans them into place in the second and third row: a pack each of Peek Freans, Lemon Crisp, Digestives, Arrowroot, Fruit Creme, Nice, Shortcake, and two packs each of Dad's Oatmeal and Oreo cookies.

She notices one of the Dad's cookies has a tear in the wrapper. Once the boxes have moved down the line, she rips the package open, popping a cookie in her mouth whole. She wonders if she and Marlene could be friends, if Marlene wants friends. Cheeks full, she doesn't swallow, and waits for Marlene to stop fussing with her net and look her way so she can test the waters by opening wide.

READER

Caucasian female, late 30s, with short, spiky blond hair, wearing baggy jeans, brown sneakers, and grey hoodie under secondhand orange, blue, and yellow ski vest.

We Need to Talk About Kevin
Lionel Shriver
(Harper Perennial, 2006)
P 56

The Curious Collector

When her son was young, he was a collector of curious objects. While her daughter combed the beach for long, slender cone shells and heart-shaped rocks, he was drawn to the oddities of imperfect fruit and vegetables — samples of which he kept in foul-smelling plastic bins she discovered during her weekly vacuum — skinned tennis balls, and placemats from the local Chinese restaurant signed and dated by the wait staff.

One morning, she began to wonder if he'd moved on to yet another hobby when she came across a dragonfly that had died on their back deck. A small wooden cross had been erected beside its body. Before she could remove it, her son pushed past her, his Polaroid camera poised. He took the picture, pulling the tab and counting down. "I love the light of early dawn," he said, kicking the dragonfly between the wooden slats.

READER

Caucasian female, early 60s, with short blond hair,
wearing glasses, tan coat, white collared shirt,
and pale green silk scarf.

The Sweet Edge
Alison Pick
(Raincoast Books, 2005)
P 153

Sailor

They walk together down the beach. She could be as young as ten, he thinks, certainly no older than thirteen, which would be a six-year age difference. He flattens his part and tells her about life on a boat. The other vacationers flap the sand out of their blankets, heading up for dinner. He asks if she's in a hurry. Does she have to be somewhere?

He can't look away from her sea-green eyes, her sun-kissed nose, last week's burn beginning to flake from her chest. He's disturbed to think she might remind him a little of his baby sister.

He flattens his part again and grabs her hand, turning it palm up. Pressing a point on her wrist, he tells her that he's heard that if he keeps pressing she'll go limp in just thirty seconds. She freezes, holding his gaze. Her knees start to buckle at the twenty-second mark. He's not even doing anything, he thinks. But as the girl crumples to the sand, he drops her arm and pushes his hands into his pockets, looking to see if they've been spotted. It's just a mind trick, he says to himself. He's done nothing wrong.

READER

Caucasian female, early 20s, with short brown hair
and hoop earrings, wearing long, dark overcoat and
green scarf, book bag slung over shoulder.

The Bell Jar
Sylvia Plath
(Faber and Faber, 1966)
P 127

Reception

Her job was to wait below while he climbed the TV antenna tower. Terry cloth shorts bunched between her chubby legs, she kept a lookout for adults, siblings, the school principal who lived next door, anyone with sense enough to call his parents. He would be quick. By his rules of the game, only once up and down constituted a closed case. Then they could retreat to the basement, where they would lie on the couch, "getting the girl" his reward for another mystery solved.

READER

Caucasian male, mid-30s, with full beard, wearing black dress pants, blue dress shirt, with sleeves rolled to elbows, and scuffed leather shoes.

The Amazing Adventures of Kavalier and Clay
Michael Chabon
(Picador, 2001)
P 72

Like Mother, Like Son

Mother: Look at your cousin Tess over at the crab dip. Girl looks like she could cry.

Son: Gran choked on a strawberry seed, you know. She's still in the washroom.

Mother: How does someone choke on a strawberry seed?

Son: Exactly. Don't eat strawberries.

Mother: Oh God, look. Tess is going for more dip.

Son: She needs to master the dip. I hear it's one of the steps.

Mother: No, I think you have to call someone and tell them you love them.

Son: Anyone?

Mother: I really don't understand how Gran can choke on something the size of a seed.

Son: She likes the attention.

Mother: Why is your father standing over by the hedges?

Son: Why is your husband standing over by the hedges?

Mother: Is he smoking? How old is that girl he's with? Is that your second cousin?

Son: Jocelyn? Janice? It's "J" something. She's really grown up. You should go get your husband.

Mother: You should go get your father. People will talk.

READER

Caucasian female, mid-50s, with blond bob, wearing purple overcoat with poppy, carrying nylon thatched bag bearing a crest of an old leather golf bag.

The Outstretched Shadow:
The Obsidian Trilogy, Book One
Mercedes Lackey and James Mallory
(Tor Books, 2004)
P 76

Glory, Glory

In the church basement, the three young teens took a break from their puppet rehearsal, one song away from calling it a night. Despite the lingering smell of adhesive, one puppet's moustache had fallen off, and another's hair, brown yarn, required a touch-up.

While the troupe's leader went up to the chapel for glue, the teens' minds turned to games, the basement equipped with a basketball court and hockey nets. They rummaged through storage and found gear: gym mats, hockey sticks, hard orange balls.

As he was retreating to the closet in search of a Nerf football, she pulled the pastor's son close. She wasn't very popular. Her hair was short and greasy. She wore purple velvet knickers, a starched white blouse with frilly collar, and oversized leggings bunched at the ankles. However, the tetracycline had done wonders to her skin, and she'd always had pretty eyes. He, meanwhile, was a grade younger. The mole on his neck thumped as she leaned against him. His hair was parted firmly down the middle, cut to the rim of the smallest serving bowl reserved for pudding and his monthly trim. He wore black corduroys and a white baseball T with burgundy sleeves. His skin was dotted with whiteheads and his eyes were set just a little too far apart.

She put her hand on his crotch and told him to open his mouth so she could kiss him. He obliged, forgetting to breathe, his head spinning when the group's leader started the music for their next number.

Rise and shine and give God the glory, glory.

 SEEN READING Julie Wilson

READER

Asian female, late 20s, black hair twisted into ponytail,
wearing grey overcoat and high-heeled suede boots,
her bookmark a worn postcard of Jupiter.

Walk in the Light & Twenty-Three Tales
Leo Tolstoy
(Orbis Books, 2003)
P 235

Rumble Row

She grew up in a shabby, narrow house on the wrong side of the track. Twice a day, once very early in the morning and again in the late afternoon, a cargo train rolled down the middle of her street, curving at the very end to cut through her backyard. The track had been built to go around her parents' house, the only people on the street who'd refused to sell. Now twice a day, a train rolled by her bedroom window, a novelty that once made her popular among her classmates. But after the novelty wore off, the children no longer visited. She stood by the window — the girl on the wrong side of the track — while the pane rattled, and she waved somberly. Some days, the conductor waved back. Most days, he pretended to ignore her. It must not be easy, she thought, driving your train through someone's backyard. Sometimes, the glass shook so violently she feared it would break. On those days, she'd press herself against the window, the vibrations tickling her deep down into her tummy, and she tried, once again, to imagine herself as the superhero who protects the world from the inevitable shards of glass, from all its injustices.

READER

Caucasian female, early 30s, wearing brown jacket, crisp blue jeans, and suede boots, black laptop bag tucked under her arm.

===

Buffy the Vampire Slayer:
The Long Way Home, Season 8, Issue 4
Joss Whedon, illustrated by Georges Jeanty, Andy Owens, Jo Chen
(Dark Horse, 2007)
near the beginning

===

Put to Pasture

The story was never told first-hand, just a family legend retold every few years when she and her mother drove out of town to pick raspberries. This stretch of road always freaks me out, is all her mother would say. The road was paved now, but some twenty years ago it was soft gravel, her grandmother a new driver like many women who only learned after their husbands left or died. It was dark, and she could expect to hit something along these roads at some point, be it deer or man. She never did stop to check.

READER

Caucasian female, mid-30s, with shoulder-length blond hair, wearing blue T-shirt, khaki capris, and leather sandals.

The Final Detail
Harlan Coben
(Island Books, 2000)
P 77

Of Age

On several occasions he's driven Trevor home, always with the intent of making sure he arrives in time to make curfew and has had plenty of water and something to line his stomach. Trevor is fifteen and wants to be a clothing designer. The owners allow minors in the bar so long as they don't drink, but what they do in the parking lot is their own business. He recognizes his own youth in Trevor's fair-haired biceps and tucked-in T-shirts. He thinks of him like a little brother, these first few months out of the closet so crucial. He considers himself Trevor's life coach — save for that first fumble in the back seat before he knew how young he was.

READER

Caucasian male, 60s, with close-cropped white hair,
wearing black leather jacket, and red, white,
and black skull cap, smoking pipe.

Lolita
Vladimir Nabokov
(Vintage, 1991)
near end

When You Least Expect It

When you least expect it, he's been told. Stop looking and when you least expect it. He stares out the window counting house numbers, a game he's played since youth. Pick a number and imagine yourself the home's owner. 458. 460. 462. The streetcar rolls past a house with a worn couch on the front porch and a stack of soaked boxes leaning in the corner. He picks another number far ahead, spends the time considering the woman who sits two seats ahead reading a new paperback, something with a mustard cover. He'll look out for it, the book with the mustard cover. 1236. When the house appears, its tidy front lawn is dotted with trees. Is that a Japanese maple? What does he know about trees? He looks again at the reader who pulls a stray hair behind her ear, her finger hovering by her lobe as if she's forgotten to lower her arm, because she has. Yes, he thinks, the trees could be her job. And the kids can rake the leaves while he stirs the milk for hot chocolate.

READER

Caucasian male, mid-30s, with short blond hair,
wearing a green hooded jacket, brown leather shoes,
and deeply creased black jeans.

───

The Blue Light Project
Timothy Taylor
(Knopf, 2011)
p 246

───

Secret Santa

Champagne and orange juice, the gateway cocktail, she thought as the new office admin hurried about the kitchenette. Everyone was on their second round of mimosas, but she politely rejected his offer of a top up. How old was he, anyhow — twelve? Should he even be handling alcohol? She looked at the clock and timed how long she'd have to endure small talk with virtual strangers, until her holiday could officially begin. Three hours. Christ Almighty. Most of her co-workers who she actually liked — who liked her — had booked off early, leaving her to suffer through Secret Santa with the knowledge that of the four remaining staff, at least two seemed to genuinely loathe her, and one, well, at least they could look each other in the eye again after that faulty lock incident in the washroom.

The admin dangled a small gift bag in front of her, the tag left blank. "There was a mix-up with the names," he whispered. "But, we didn't want you to go home empty-handed." He smiled. His teeth are the colour of first snow, she thought, folding her lips into a flat grin.

As the others tore into their presents, she pulled a tiny gorilla key chain from the bag, a wad of tissue paper falling to the floor. She pressed a button on the gorilla's belly, a fond memory rushing forward of a stuffed monkey she'd had as a child that yodelled when you poked its chest. The gorilla's eyes flashed a blinding blue, its screech cutting through the din of conversation. Her co-workers stopped to look in her direction. If she could will herself to laugh right now, they might believe she was actually enjoying herself.

READER

Caucasian woman, mid-30s, with long blond hair,
wearing black, floor-length wool coat and grey knit hat
with two large wooden buttons on the side.

═══

The Waterproof Bible
Andrew Kaufman
(Random House Canada, 2010)
P 75

═══

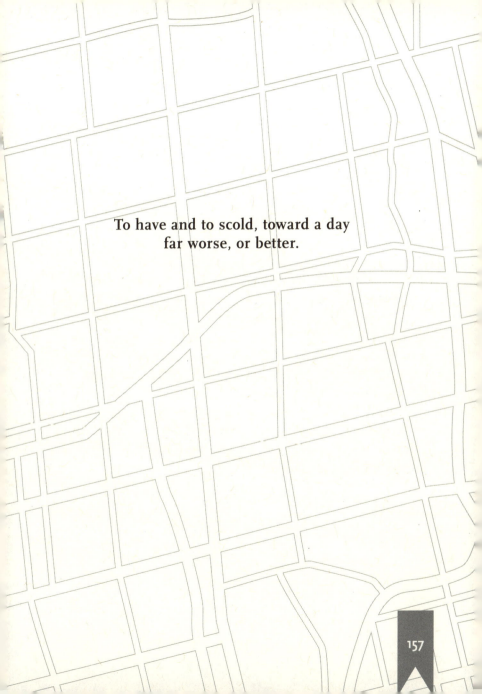
To have and to scold, toward a day far worse, or better.

XXX-XXX-XXXX

He removes his glasses and rubs his eyes, pinching the bridge of his nose and sighing. He lets his head fall, chin to his chest, book falling open limp on his knee. He shifts a bit and rights himself, squinting at an ad across the aisle. He reads everything. Posters. Logos. He nods, not necessarily because he agrees. It could be that he's remembering, some past conversation, maybe from this morning, more likely from late the night before. He shakes his head. His point wasn't taken. He puts his glasses back on, and cocks his head to the side, taking in the contents under the seat adjacent to him: a Fairlee bottle emptied of its 100% Pure/Pur orange juice from concentrate. He swivels to look overhead. Call us at xxx-xxx-xxxx. His lips never stop moving.

READER

Caucasian male, early 20s, with short brown hair and thin sideburns, wearing glasses with red frames, grey coat, jet-black jeans, and charcoal slip-on Vans.

Fruit
Brian Francis
(ECW Press, 2004)
P 47

Monsters in the Bones

When she came to, a homeless man was standing over her. She'd fallen from her bike. It had been a bad fall. The damn tracks grabbed her tire. Gonna have monsters in the bones for a good long time, the man said. But you take this, the offer of a loonie extended from his dirty fingers. He let the coin drop awkwardly onto her chest. The coffee shop will let you stay for an hour if you buy a cup.

READER

Caucasian female, mid-20s, with brown hair loosely pulled into a ponytail, wearing jade earrings, pink racerback tank top, black yoga capris, thick wool socks, hiking shoes, and nose ring.

———

The Gabriel Hounds
Mary Stewart
(HarperTorch, 2006)
p 68

———

Wedding Dress

He stands alone in his grandmother's bedroom, collecting bags of dead batteries, used Kleenex balls, and loose safety pins from her side table. Her bed still holds the indent of her form. He lies in the depression, facing the window to see what she would have seen, listening to the chatter coming from the schoolyard outside.

She'd taken his hand and rubbed it over her lower stomach. "Can you feel it? It's massive." She'd gotten so tiny, half her size, small enough to fit into her wedding dress again. Said she'd taken it out from storage, the tiring task of putting it on consuming the morning and two pots of tea. Finally, standing in front of her mirror, she saw herself sixty years earlier; she would begin to raise their four children alone. She'd undressed, rolled the gown into a ball, and gone out into the hall in her stocking feet to thrust it down the garbage chute.

He gets out of the bed, back to the chore of removing dried masking tape from her wardrobe mirror, the years of Christmas and birthday cards packed into a fresh large envelope purchased from the drugstore on the corner.

READER

Caucasian female, mid-20s, with brown curly hair pulled back in clip, wearing vest, knitted sweater, long jean skirt, thick stockings, and hiking boots.

The Girls' Guide to Hunting and Fishing
Melissa Bank
(Penguin, 2000)
P 220

Wearing Her Indoor Face

She forgot, and now she's wearing her indoor lipstick outside. The filter of her cigarette is stained bright orange. Five more minutes on the last load of drying and she can get out of here.

She forgot, and now her lips ablaze with long-lasting metallic pearl. She's afraid she'll see someone she knows and they'll ask after her and she'll have to say, No, no she passed on. So young, they'll say, their eyes stuck on her lips. Yes, she'll say, straightening the length of her jacket. Yes, she was far too young. God bless, they'll say.

Her daughter was so pale and small, but the therapist said she was ready for visitors. She'd gone to the store not knowing what girls her age like these days. She herself had only ever worn one shade of red. Looking lost at the counter, she'd let a young woman around the same age as her daughter show her samples. I don't know what she likes, she'd said. She looks different every week. She'd bought the lot, approaching the hospital room with her shopping bag full. It was cause for celebration, a whole spoonful of oatmeal.

She'd been raised not to waste money, so she saved the lipsticks in her daughter's Hello Kitty make-up case, rising each morning to put on the kettle, the FM radio, and her indoor lipstick.

But today she forgot, and now she's out in the world, and it's written all over her face.

READER

Caucasian female, 50s, with curly black hair
and orange lips, wearing black wool coat
and patterned silk scarf.

Fables of Brunswick Avenue
Katherine Govier
(Harper Perennial, 2005)
P 155

Pricks

She sat on the edge of the schoolyard. While football players ran through tires and sprinted the length of the field, she drew a thick ankh in black Sharpie across her pale ankle. She pulled her black hood forward over her face so even the tiniest sliver of sunshine couldn't graze her cheeks.

This is where they'd made out for the first time, skipping out on rehearsal for the school musical. Coming to grind against one another on the cold ground, unchaperoned.

Now, he wanted to meet, to talk, his text had said. She rolled the piercing in her tongue. This morning, she saw him laughing in the hall, opening his mouth so The Soprano could touch his matching piercing. She took a swig from her Listerine, and tossed the empty into the brush. Jesus H., she swore, and retrieved the bottle to recycle later. She jumped, refusing to look at him, when he announced his arrival by kicking the sole of her combat boot.

You will not cry. You will not cry.

READER

Caucasian female, early 20s, wearing
sleek black coat, collar high.

Brick Lane
Monica Ali
(Scribner, 2004)
P 275

Counting Cars

His great-aunt takes a sip of white wine, her eyes rounding into saucers.

He's not sure what she heard him say. He leans forward, sorts through the crystal bowl of nuts set out for visitors, picking out the cashews, dividing the neglected Brazil nuts and pecans into a fresh heap. He leans back into the floral couch with a groan, rolling the nuts in his palm like dice before dealing each one into his mouth.

Her lips tighten into a small opening, her breath a steady whistle. She shakes her head slightly, brow creased. She takes another sip of wine as she rearranges the shortbread on the chipped china plate. Looking out the kitchen window, she counts the cars of a cargo train that has started to steam by outside.

Up to one hundred, how wonderful. She turns to her handsome young groom. One hundred, darling, how wonderful. She considers the fine lines of his cheekbones. Wonderful.

READER

Caucasian female, late 60s, wearing pink tank top,
and white shorts.

———

Missing Mom
Joyce Carol Oates
(Ecco, 2006)
P 35

———

Procession

The only time she was alone with her best friend's father was the day he hoisted her bike into the wide trunk of his Cadillac and drove her back over the tracks, up the long, unfinished drive to her home. They arrived just as her mother was about to lock the screen door for the night. Her mother pinched her robe closed at the neck. His smile offered explanation; her mother's offered apology. His hand ushered the girl over the threshold with a final pat.

Your best friend lives next door, across the street, occasionally two yards behind you. Your best friend can be in your class, but it's not mandatory. Street rules: a ten-year-old and a seven-year-old have enough in common if all they do is toss a ball in the street until dinner's called. And if parents are willing to take in the mail while the other's out of town, best friends are pretty much forced upon one another.

This boy, though, had lived a bike ride away — a twenty-three minute ride, to be exact — on the other side of a bridge. Twelve and eleven, they had somehow found the other. Together, they scavenged ravines and stood watch across the street from the funeral parlour, grasping each other's hand tightly, boasting they weren't afraid of death.

READER

Caucasian woman, late 20s, with long brown hair in hairband, wearing tan skirt, white tank top, and pistachio-green sweater.

Mistress of the Sun
Sandra Gulland
(HarperCollins, 2008)
P 217

The Birth of a Handsome Nose

She was nine years old. The kitchen linoleum slid under her sockettes like ice, her ankles strong, balance pegged. Not the most graceful dancer, but with each glide her confidence grew. She shouldered her weight across the counter, bracing herself into a scissor-kick lift, chin grazing the breadbox.

When she landed, it was with a dull thud. She thought she heard something creaking, a trail of blood creeping along a fissured bridge. Left in place, the doctors took the chance it would straighten.

Three years later on a volleyball court, she stepped up to the net, the game-losing spike blocked: the final blow. Yet, the birth of a handsome nose.

READER

Asian female, early 30s, with broad shoulders,
wavy hair bunched up high, wearing black
v-neck cotton shirt.

———

Dusk Dances 2007
Withrow Park, Toronto
P 97

———

Pink

There are syrupy bumps on the back of her pink bathroom door buried under multiple coats of paint. They've been there since she moved in; who knows how long before that. The bumps remind her of her grandmother, the hinges on her pink bathroom door painted so many times it barely shut. She leans forward on the toilet and delicately traces the bumps with her finger. Just two pink bathroom doors in a long line of pink bathroom doors.

READER

Caucasian female, early 20s, wearing low-slung white jeans, white puffy jacket, French tips, and UGGs.

═══

The Tipping Point
Malcolm Gladwell
(Little, Brown and Company, 2000)
P 82

═══

Hero

He comes in the same time each day, reads in the back corner for hours until he pulls out a journal into which he doodles madly. She refills his coffee, piling fresh creamers beside his pens and watercolours. Occasionally he stands, walking up and down the aisle between the mostly empty booths, on the balls of his feet, hands shoved into the high pockets of his khaki floods. Bottom lip stuck out, he doesn't sit until he's reached some conclusion, a thought he punctuates with a salute and a click of his heels to no one in particular. His short curls are matted down from sleep, he doesn't always smell very nice, and his teeth protrude a little, but she's certain that in his story, he's the hero and gets all the girls.

READER

East Indian female, early 30s, with long black hair,
wearing purple velvet coat, long black skirt,
and thick-soled boots.

═

Brown Girl in the Ring
Nalo Hopkinson
(Grand Central Publishing, 2007)
P 174

═

Holding

He was sitting on the couch holding the phone to his ear when his wife strode in with the groceries. He nodded once and continued to flip through a magazine. Minutes later, he held the receiver away from his ear, the cursing on the other end of the line heard well into the kitchen where his wife stood over a steeping tea bag, hands planted firmly on the counter. "How long have you been on this time?" she murmured so quietly it was as if to herself. "An hour. Mum's just forgotten where she is again," he replied, and then, assuringly, "but she'll get back," as if to himself. "What, darling?" his wife said from the kitchen.

READER

South Asian male, with short brown hair and labret piercing, wearing glasses, grey hoodie under black fleece, low black jeans, and black Converse sneakers.

Atmospheric Disturbances
Rivka Galchen
(HarperCollins, 2008)
p 63

Twisty Ties

The woman beside her wants to talk. She wonders aloud, are these cars air conditioned? Should she have brought a jacket?

This woman hugs a small suitcase to her knees, a white leather purse with ball point scribbles along one seam stuffed in her lap. Her son sits across from her, his suitcase closing him in. He rests his head on top of it, one earphone in, the other dangling, emitting the steady beats of hip hop.

"You forgot to put the twisty ties on the zippers," the woman calls to her son.

He lifts his head, shrugs.

"I didn't buy you no new shorts and T-shirts to have somebody steal 'em."

"Ma," the boy mumbles. "Twisty ties ain't gonna keep nobody out of this luggage if they want to get into this luggage."

"Every bit helps," she says, looking at her neighbour again. "You have kids," the woman says, not so much a question as a statement. "They don't know until they got to pay for it themselves."

"Maybe," she responds, turning the page of her book.

"Ma," the boy grumbles.

"Maybe. Maybe not. But, one day, somebody's gonna take something from you, and then you'll know. Every chance, we got to try."

READER

Black woman, early 40s, wearing white sleeveless shirt,
grey dress capris, thick-soled black sneakers,
carrying turquoise leather purse.

―――

Sweeter Than Honey
Mary B. Morrison
(Kensington, 2009)
P 56

―――

Authors Note: Publication dates and publishers provided refer to the sighted edition of each book, not necessarily the text's original publication date or original publisher.

Ali, Monica. *Brick Lane* (Scribner, 2004). "Pricks," page 166

Alliott, Catherine. *Not That Kind of Girl* (Headline Book Publishing, 2005). "House Rules," page 27

Atwood, Margaret. *Payback* (House of Anansi Press, 2008). "Sticks and Twigs," page 94

Baldacci, David. *Total Control* (Grand Central Publishing, 1997). "Dreams of a Would-Be Government Employee," page 44

Bank, Melissa. *The Girls' Guide to Hunting and Fishing* (Penguin, 2000). "Wedding Dress," page 162

Bellow, Saul. *Herzog* (Penguin, 2003). "Miss Popular," page 54

Bergen, David. *The Retreat* (McClelland & Stewart, 2008). "Breaking Ties," page 26

Bergen, David. *The Time in Between* (McClelland & Stewart, 2005). "Legal Limits," page 20

Bloom, Amy. *A Blind Man Can See How Much I Love You* (Random House, 2000). "Morning Glories," page 30

Bock, Dennis. *The Communist's Daughter* (HarperCollins, 2007). "Riding the Rails," page 56

Boyden, Joseph. *Three Day Road* (Penguin Canada, 2008). "Indiana Summers," page 104

Boyden, Joseph. *Through Black Spruce* (Penguin Canada, 2009). "Visitor," page 114

Brainard, Joe. *I Remember* (Granary Books, 2001). "After Joe Brainard," page 4

Brooks, Max. *World War Z: An Oral History of the Zombie War* (Three Rivers Press, 2007). "Intrusion," page 96

Bronte, Emily. *Wuthering Heights* (Dover, 1996). "Clearcutting," page 68

Burke, Alafair. *Close Case* (St. Martin's Press, 2006). "Side Tables," page 90

Chabon, Michael. *The Amazing Adventures of Kavalier and Clay* (Picador, 2001). "Reception," page 140

Coady, Lynn. *Mean Boy* (Anchor Canada, 2006). "Winter Wonderland," page 102

Coben, Harlan. *The Final Detail* (Island Books, 2000). "Put to Pasture," page 148

Cohen, Tish. *Town House* (HarperCollins, 2007). "Pillow Talk," page 60

Dawkins, Richard. *The God Delusion* (Houghton Mifflin Harcourt, 2008). "Grace," page 128

Desai, Kiran. *The Inheritance of Loss* (Penguin Canada, 2006). "Undertow," page 6

Dessen, Sarah. *The Truth About Forever* (Penguin, 2006). "The Young Lovers, Part II," page 76

Dostoevsky, Fyodor. *Crime and Punishment* (Dover, 2001). "Mercy," page 66

Dusk Dances 2007, Toronto, Withrow Park. "The Birth of a Handsome Nose," page 172

Eugenides, Jeffrey. *Middlesex* (Knopf, 2003). "(In)digestion," page 18

Feynman, Richard P. *The Pleasure of Finding Things Out: The Best Short Works of Richard P. Feynman* (Basic, 2005). "Jelly," page 110

Foran, Charles. *Mordecai, The Life & Times* (Knopf, 2010). "Simple Sandwiches," page 46

Francis, Brian. *Fruit* (ECW Press, 2004). "XXX-XXX-XXXX," page 158

Galchen, Rivka. *Atmospheric Disturbances* (HarperCollins, 2008). "Holding," page 178

Gibb, Camilla. *The Beauty of Humanity Movement* (Doubleday Canada, 2010). "Flat," page 88

Giffin, Emily. *Baby Proof* (St. Martins Press, 2006). "Pinhead," page 106

Gladwell, Malcolm. *The Tipping Point* (Little, Brown and Company, 2000). "Pink," page 174

Govier, Katherine. *Fables of Brunswick Avenue* (HarperPerennial, 2005). "Wearing Her Indoor Face," page 164

Groopman, Jerome. *How Doctors Think* (Houghton Mifflin Harcourt, 2008). "Love Will Tear Us Apart," page 84

Gulland, Sandra. *Mistress of the Sun* (HarperCollins, 2008). "Procession," page 170

Heti, Sheila. *Ticknor* (House of Anansi Press, 2005). "Small Talks," page 38

Hiaasen, Carl. *Star Island* (Knopf, 2010). "Cherry," page 82

Highsmith, Patricia. *The Selected Stories of Patricia Highsmith* (Norton, 2001). "Girl's Dorm," page 10

Hill, Lawrence. *The Book of Negroes* (HarperCollins, 2007). "Woman and Parrot," page 42

Hopkinson, Nalo. *Brown Girl in the Ring* (Grand Central Publishing, 2007). "Hero," page 176

Horn, Dara. *The World to Come* (Norton, 2006). "Tin Can," page 2

Hosseini, Khaled. *The Kite Runner* (Anchor Canada, 2004). "Ends," page 74

July, Miranda. *No One Belongs Here More Than You* (Scribner, 2008). "The Health Hustle," page 62

Kaufman, Andrew. *The Waterproof Bible* (Random House Canada, 2010). "Secret Santa," page 154

King, Stephen. *Misery* (Signet, 2010). "Simmer," page 98

Krakauer, Jon. *Into the Wild* (Anchor, 1997). "Creature Feature," page 130

Lackey, Mercedes and Mallory, James. *The Outstretched Shadow: The Obsidian Trilogy*, Book One (Tor Books, 2004). "Like Mother, Like Son," page 142

Manguel, Alberto. *The City of Words* (House of Anansi Press, 2007). "Irlsgay," page 118

McCarthy, Cormac. *Blood Meridian* (Vintage, 1992). "Complementary Colours," page 34

Morrison, Mary B. *Sweeter Than Honey* (Kensington, 2009). "Twisty Ties," page 180

Nabokov, Vladimir. *Lolita* (Vintage, 1991). "Of Age," page 150

Ngozi, Chimamanda Adichie. *Half of a Yellow Sun* (Vintage, 2007). "Divorced Before 30," page 86

Nix, Garth. Biggs, Brian (Illustrator). *One Beastly Beast* (HarperCollins, 2007). "Bagged Lunch," page 52

Oates, Joyce Carol. *Missing Mom* (Ecco, 2006). "Counting Cars," page 168

Palahniuk, Chuck. *Choke* (Anchor, 2002). "Biopsy," page 80

Patchett, Ann. *Bel Canto* (HarperCollins, 2005). "A Quick Peek," page 12

Pick, Alison. *The Sweet Edge* (Raincoast Books, 2005). "The Curious Collector," page 136

Plath, Sylvia. *The Bell Jar* (Faber and Faber, 1966). "Sailor," page 138

Quarrington, Paul. *King Leary* (Anchor Books, 2007). "One Boy In," page 14

Quiviger, Pascale. Fischman, Sheila (Translator) *The Perfect Circle* (Cormorant Books, 2006). "Cherry Tree," page 8

Reed, Alan. *Isobel and Emile* (Coach House Books, 2010). "He Didn't See It Coming," page 22

Ricci, Nino. *The Origin of Species* (Doubleday, 2008). "Esther," page 124

Ricci, Nino. *The Origin of Species* (Doubleday, 2008). "Swedish Berries," page 64

Roach, Mary. *Spook: Science Tackles the Afterlife* (Norton, 2005). "Tho. Shelton," page 36

Roach, Mary. *Stiff* (Norton, 2004). "'86," page 108

Rowling. J.K. *Harry Potter and the Deathly Hallows* (Raincoast, 2007). "Cursive," page 100

Shriver, Lionel. *We Need to Talk About Kevin* (Harper Perennial, 2006). "Girlfriends," page 134

Sim, Dave. Gerhard (Illustrator). *Cerebus #300* (Aardvark-Vanaheim, 2004). "The Young Lovers, Part I," page 76

Smart, Elizabeth. *By Grand Central Station I Sat Down and Wept* (HarperCollins, 1991). "Six Spin," page 28

Smith, Ali. *The Whole Story and other stories* (Hamish Hamilton, 2003). "Love Noted," page 72

Stern, Jerome (Editor). *Micro Fiction: An Anthology of Really Short Stories* (Norton, 1996). "A Room of His Own," page 120

Stewart, Mary. *The Gabriel Hounds* (HarperTorch, 2006). "Monsters in the Bones," page 160

Taylor, Timothy. *The Blue Light Project* (Knopf, 2011). "When You Least Expect It," page 152

Tolstoy, Leo. *Walk in the Light & Twenty-Three Tales* (Orbis Books, 2003). "Glory, Glory," page 144

Vassanji, M.G. *The Book of Secrets* (McClelland & Stewart, 1994). "If This Buick Could Talk," page 126

Vonnegut, Kurt. *Slaughterhouse-Five* (Dial Press Trade Paperback, 1999). "It Begins the Same," page 58

Walls, Jeannette. *The Glass Castle* (Scribner, 2006). "Dress Rehearsal," page 16

Walls, Jeannette. *The Glass Castle* (Scribner, 2006). "Red," page 112

Wells, H.G. *The Time Machine* (Phoenix Pick, 2008). "Sugar Bowls," page 122

Whedon, Joss. Jeanty, Georges. Owens, Andy. Chen, Jo. (Illustrators). *Buffy the Vampire Slayer: The Long Way Home*, Season 8, Issue 4 (Dark Horse, 2007). "Rumble Row," page 146

Woods, Sherryl. *Feels Like Family* (Mira, 2010). "Lots and Lots," page 40

Wurtzel, Elizabeth. *Prozac Nation* (Houghton Mifflin, 1994). "Surplus," page 36

Acknowledgements

To all literary voyeurs and exhibitionist readers; to every writer who has enhanced my world or the way in which I live in it (and to their publishers); to booksellers; and to my family, born and borrowed.

With love and thanks to Jill Purdy, Dani Couture, Mary Brindle, Sean Cranbury, and Amy Logan Holmes for laughter, life and lessons; to George Murray and Ashley Winnington-Ball, *Seen Reading*'s fire-starters; and, to Sarah MacLachlan, Lynn Henry, and my old cohorts at House of Anansi Press for playing such a significant role in my coming out as a professional publishing fan.

With appreciation to the Toronto Transit Commission for the workspace, and the Ontario Arts Council for the financial support.

With great affection to my agent Samantha Haywood and my editor Robyn Read for trusting in these tiny fictions; to Sarah Ivany and her boundless belief in the writers and books she publicizes; and, to Natalie Olsen for her gorgeous preoccupation with book design.

Lastly, to my first reader, the nameless woman at The Old Nick, and to my dear chum Kristine Lukanchoff for running a pub in which readers will always feel welcome.

To see early versions of these stories in their original context, please visit www.seenreading.com.

This book was printed on 80lb Mohawk Loop Feltmark Natural and 60lb Rolland Opaque Natural. It was set in ff Scala and the accompanying sans serif designed by Martin Majoor. The display face is Toronto Street Sign and was created by Dave Murray based on the weathered lettering on the classic black-and-white signs.

JULIE WILSON

Julie Wilson is The Book Madam, a self-professed "professional publishing fan" living and working in Toronto. She's the past Online Marketing Manager for House of Anansi Press and recent Host of the CBC Book Club. She thinks reading looks good on you. Follow Julie on Twitter: @**BookMadam** and @**SeenReading**. Post your own reader sightings using the hashtag #seenreading.

ING BLACK LIPSTICK, AND BEARD HAIR WITH STU... READER: CAUCASIAN FEMALE, LATE 30S, WITH SH... BLACK HAIR AND REDDISH HAIR, LATE 40S, WEARING PATTERNED... READER: CAUCASIAN FEMALE, LATE 30S, WITH... WITH SHORT BLACK FABRIC, LATE 40S, AND SANDALS. READER: CAUCASIAN FEMALE, MIDS 20S, WITH... CAUCASIAN FEMALE, LATE 40S, AND BLACK TURTLENECK SWEATER, MID 20S, WITH SHORT BLACK... WITH SHORT GREEN PETAL FLOATING WHITE LEATHER JACKET, MIDS 20S, WITH BROWN... READER: ASIAN CAUCASIAN MALE, MIDS 20S, WITH BROWN PETAL SHORTS, CAUCASIAN FEMALE, MID 20S, WITH... READER: ASIAN CAUCASIAN MALE, LATE 20S, WITH BRIGHT... BOOK ENCASED IN GREY SHORTS, READER: ASIAN CAUCASIAN MALE, LATE 20S, WITH MID 20S, WITH... READER: CAUCASIAN MALE, LATE 20S, WEARING PLAIN WHITE JEAN JACKET WITH FLOWER PETAL... BURGUNDY T-SHIRT, GREY SCARF, WEARING JEAN JACKET WITH MID 20S, WITH LONG BLONDE HAIR PU... HOODIE, AND LIGHT SCARF, FRESHLY WASHED PONYTAIL CAP. READER: CAUCASIAN MALE, LATE 20S, WITH LONG BLONDE HAIR P... SCARF, AND GLASS BAUBLE RING ON LAP. READER: CAUCASIAN MALE, LATE 20S, WITH LONG DARK HAIR SHO... NATIVE CANADIAN FEMALE, MID 20S, WEARING WITH A THICK CORDUROY CAP. READER: CAUCASIAN MALE, LATE 20S, WITH LONG DARK HAIR SHO... PULLED BACK IN NEAT, FRESHLY HOISTED ON BLACK CORDUROY CAP. READER: CAUCASIAN MALE, LATE 20S, WITH LONG BLONDE JEANS, AND... EARS, WEARING BLACK AND LEATHER CARRY-ALL HOISTED UP. READER: CAUCASIAN MALE, 60S, WITH LONG BLOND JEANS, SOUTH ASIAN... BLACK PANTS, AND SLICK LIP GLOSS. COLLAR UP, READER: CAUCASIAN MALE, 60S, WITH LONG BEARD... CARGO PANTS, AND SLICK LIP GLOSS. READER: CAUCASIAN FEMALE, LATE 20S, WITH LONG BEARD. READER: IN MID... BLACK CAP, WHITE DRESS SHIRT, AND GREY TWEED COAT. COLLAR UP, LATE 20S, WITH LONG BEARD. READER: IN MID... BLACK CAP, RED GLASSES, AND LEATHER SLIPPERS. READER: CAUCASIAN FEMALE, 60S, WITH LONG HAIR PARTED DOWN THE MIDDLE... SWEATER AND HAT, LARGE LEATHER SLIPPERS. READER: CAUCASIAN MALE, FADED JEANS, AND... TUCKED INTO KNITTED CAP, AND BLACK POOL SLIDE SANDALS. READER: CAUCASIAN FEMALE, CAUCASIAN MA... BLACK JEANS, BLACK TURTLENECK, AND GREY DRESS JACKET. READER: CAUCASIAN FEMALE, FADED DOWN... TUCKED SWEATER, GREY SCARF, AND LEATHER SLIPPERS. READER: CAUCASIAN FEMALE, CAU... DED SHORTS, BLACK JACKET, BLACK JEANS, WEARING GREEN JACKET WITH RED AND WHITE CROSS-STITCHING ON... GO HOODIE, PINSTRIPED SUIT JACKET, FADED JEANS, AND WHITE CROSS-STITCHING ON... SKIRT, WEARING BLACK HAIR, EARLY 50S, WEARING RED JEANS AND WHITE SNEAKERS. READER: CAUCAS... BUTTON DOWN EVERY FEW MINUTES TO CRACK HIS KNUCKLES AND LOOK OUT THE WINDOW. READER: CAUCAS... CURLY, SHOULDER-LENGTH, LIGHT BLUE HOODIE, CAUCASIAN MALE, EARLY 20S, WITH MULTIPLE FACIAL PIERCINGS, WEAR... THE BOOK PINNED ON NORTH FACE JACKET, AND GREY HOODIE UNDER SECON... WEARING BLUE KNIT CAP, LIGHT BLUE HOODIE, CAUCASIAN FEMALE, BROWN SNEAKERS, AND GREY HOODIE UNDER SECON... BUTTON DOWN SPIKY BLONDE HAIR, WEARING COLLARED SHIRT, DARK RUNNING SCARF, READER: CAUC... HOLES. PINNED ON NORTH FACE JACKET. READER: CAUCASIAN FEMALE, BROWN SILK SCARF, READER: CAUC... WITH SHORT BEARD, WEARING HOOP EARRINGS, BLUE JEANS, WEARING COLLARED SHIRT, DARK RUNNING SHOES. BLUE DRESS... AND YELLOW SKI VEST, TEAL LEGGINGS, AND HIGH HEELED SUEDE BOOTS. HER BAG. BOOKMARK IS... FINGERLESS GREEN GLOVES, TAN COAT, WITH FULL BEARD, IMAGE OF OLD LEATHER DRESS PANTS, BLUE DRESS... COAT, BLUE AND BROWN HAIR AND HOOP EARRINGS, AND PALE CAUCASIAN FEMALE, MID 30S, DRESS PANTS, BL... BLONDE HAIR, WEARING GLASSES, EARLY 30S, WEARING WEARING BROWN JACKET WITH BLONDE BOB, BOOKMARK IS A... COAT, WITH SHORT BLACK SUEDE LEATHER SHOES. READER: CAUCASIAN MALE, MID 50S, CRISP BLUE JEANS, AND S... SHOULDER, AND SCUFFED BROWN HAIR AND BLACK LEATHER SHOES. READER: CAUCASIAN MALE, MID 50S, CRISP BLUE JEANS, AND S... COAT TO ELBOWS, CARRYING NYLON THATCHED BAG BARING IMAGE OF OLD GOLF CLOSE CROPPED BLACK BEARD... 205, WITH POPPY, CARRYING NYLON OVERCOAT AND HIGHHEELED SUEDE BOOTS. CLOSE CROPPED BLACK HAT WI... COAT WITH PONYTAIL, CAUCASIAN FEMALE, EARLY 30S, WITH SHOULDER LENGTH BLOND HA... BAG TWISTED INTO PONYTAIL, CAUCASIAN MALE, SMOKING PIPE. READER: CAUCASIAN MALE, THIN WITH... BLACK HAIR TUCKED UNDER HER ARM. READER: CAUCASIAN MALE, SMOKING PIPE. READER: CAUCASIAN FEMALE, LAT... COAT OF JUPITER. READER: BLACK SKULL CAP, BROWN WOOL COAT AND DEEPLY-CREASED GREY KNIT HAT W... LEATHER SANDALS, AND RED, WHITE, BLACK SKULL CAP, BROWN WOOL COAT AND THIN WI... CARD HAIR, WEARING BLACK SKULL CAP, BROWN CURLY HAIR PULLED BACK YOGA CAPR... BAG HOODED JACKET, WEARING BLACK FLOOR-LENGTH SILK VANS. TANK TOP, PINK RACER BACK YOGA CAPR... LEATHER JACKET, AND CHARCOAL SLIP ON VANS. TANK TOP, PINK RACER BACK YOGA CAPR... FEMALE, MID 20S, WEARING BLACK WOOL COAT AND PATTERNED SILK ROBE READER: CAUCASIAN FEMALE, LAT... BLOND HAIR, CAUCASIAN MALE, EARLY 20S, WITH BROWN WOOL COAT AND PATTERNED SILK ROBE. READER: CAUCASIAN FEMALE, LAT... READER: CAUCASIAN MALE, WEARING JADE EARRINGS, PINK RACER BACK TANK TOP, PINK HAIR-BAT... FEMALE, HIKING BOOTS, CAUCASIAN FEMALE, MID 20S, WEARING... DRESSED IN BLACK WOOL READER: CAUCASIAN FEMALE, WITH LONG WAVY HAIR BUNCHED... HIGH, LONG BROWN HAIR, WEARING... WAVY HAIR EARLY 20S, WITH LONG...